IF ONLY THEY HAD NOT VENTURED THROUGH THAT STRANGE GATEWAY!

They would be happily examining the stars, inspecting uninhabited worlds, traveling in their peaceful, nurturing silence as they usually did. But they had foolishly gone through, and they were in this strange place, forced to learn what they could through the annoying and frightening jabbering of not just one but *dozens* of strange beings.

With no spoken language of their own, it had taken decades of their best minds working on the problem to evolve a translator that took the chatter of other races and turned it into the mental waves that the Ones Who Will Not Be Named could understand. Masters Technology now worked the controls. Finally, it was able to turn off the intrusive noise. Alien words translated into thoughts bombarded them. . . .

STAR TREK VOYAGER® GATEWAYS

BOOK FIVE OF SEVEN

NO MAN'S LAND

Christie Golden
Based upon STAR TREK®
created by Gene Roddenberry,
and STAR TREK: VOYAGER
created by Rick Berman & Michael Piller
& Jeri Taylor

POCKET BOOKS
New York   London   Toronto   Sydney   Singapore

An *Original* Publication of POCKET BOOKS

POCKET BOOKS, a division of Simon & Schuster, Inc.
1230 Avenue of the Americas, New York, NY 10020

This book is published by Pocket Books, a division of
Simon & Schuster, Inc., under exclusive license from
Paramount Pictures.

ISBN: 0-7434-1857-3

First Pocket Books printing October 2001

10 9 8 7 6 5 4 3 2 1

POCKET and colophon are registered trademarks of
Simon & Schuster, Inc.

For information regarding special discounts for bulk purchases,
please contact Simon & Schuster Special Sales at 1-800-456-6798
or business@simonandschuster.com

Printed in the U.S.A.

*This book is humbly and gratefully dedicated
to my wonderful readers,
Who now number in the hundreds of thousands.
I hope to entertain you for some time to come.
Thank you, and enjoy.*

NO MAN'S LAND

CHAPTER

1

CHAKOTAY SIGHED HEAVILY. "I HATE TO SAY IT, BUT I'm afraid it doesn't look good."

Captain Kathryn Janeway's blue gaze flickered to the face of her first officer. She didn't answer at once. When at last she spoke, her voice was heavy but resigned.

"I knew I could count on you to tell me the truth." Chakotay had only spoken aloud the suspicion that had been growing in her own gut.

Chakotay nodded solemnly. His unhappiness was plain on his handsome face. "It doesn't look good at all."

A smile crept onto Janeway's lips. "All right, no need to rub it in," she said. "Well, as they say, nothing ventured, nothing gained."

Grimly, she stepped forward and drew a cloth

1

over the abysmal painting, hiding it from view. "Into the replicator it goes."

"You did have some interesting usage of color over in the upper right-hand corner," said Chakotay.

Her smile was a full-fledged grin now. "You're backpedaling. No, it was a pretty bad effort. I guess abstract is not for me."

"It wasn't for da Vinci, either," offered Chakotay.

"And now we segue into flat-out flattery," Janeway retorted, her hands on her hips. "Are you bucking for my job, Commander?"

"When we get back I might just want a little ship of my own again."

A variety of emotions rose inside Janeway. First, and most powerful, was joy. "When" we get back, Chakotay had said. Everyone aboard *Voyager* was now substituting that hopeful, happy word for the ambiguous "if." Their brief communication with Starfleet Command, through the auspices of one Reginald Barclay, had infused the entire crew with hope. Torres had already informed Janeway that the new hyperspace technology and the modifications for the com system looked promising. There was now every reason to substitute "when" for "if."

But there was also unhappiness and apprehension commingled in that thought. Tough as things had been over the last few years, they'd faced it together, she and her crew. They'd lost some good people— and gained a few others in the forms of the remaining crew of the *Equinox* and the four Borg children. Janeway and Chakotay had grown very close. She hadn't even dared showed Tuvok the painting; she couldn't have dealt with Vulcan art criticism. Janeway could open herself to Chakotay as she could to no one else. The thought of him leaving her side, even to captain his own ship, was not one she wished to entertain overlong.

And of course, there was always the question of what kind of welcome Chakotay, B'Elanna, and the rest of the former Maquis would receive. The war was over, but she knew there were enough hawks in Starfleet Command that "forgive and forget" would likely not be the watchword of the day. From the little they had been able to gather, the Dominion War had exacted a dear cost. Some would want their pound of flesh, and with all the other Maquis safely accounted for, they might want to extract that pound from Chakotay, B'Elanna, and the others.

She'd fight for them, of course. With every ounce of strength she had in her small body.

"I hope you get that little ship, if that's what you want," Janeway said softly, impulsively reaching to squeeze his muscular forearm.

Sensing the change in her, he smiled gently. "Then again, who wants the hassles of command? It's easier being first officer."

"Barclay's changed everything, hasn't he?" She went to the replicator and ordered a cup of coffee. Turning to look at Chakotay, she inquired with a raised eyebrow if he wanted anything. He shook his head.

"Discipline has gone out the proverbial window," Chakotay said. "You've got a happy crew, but a pretty giddy one."

"Let them be a little giddy. They've been incredible. They deserve it."

"We all do."

"How is our little assimilation experiment going?" Janeway asked, sipping her coffee.

Chakotay chuckled. "Seven's doing her best, but she still doesn't think she's the best person for the job."

"Nonsense. Who better to help Borg children adapt to the challenge of individuality than a Borg who's made the journey herself? It is, as Tuvok would say, the logical choice."

"Logical doesn't always mean easy."

"I'll grant you that." Janeway thought about Chakotay's commentary on Seven's schedule for the children. "Fun" had been allotted one hour, on Seven's terms—scheduled exactly the way mealtimes, exercise, and lessons had been. And Neelix's comment about Seven's blunt statement at playtime: "Fun will now commence."

"I don't think Seven quite gets the whole fun concept," Janeway sighed.

"Sometimes I don't think her mentor does either," said Chakotay.

Janeway narrowed her eyes. "And what's that supposed to mean?"

"Exactly what it sounds like." Chakotay sat down beside her and regarded her intently. "When was the last time the captain of *Voyager* had some real fun?"

"Just last night," Janeway retorted. "I went to Fair Haven."

Chakotay was grinning. "Oh, yes," he agreed, "for all of fifteen minutes."

Caught, Janeway stalled. "Neelix wanted to see me."

"Neelix's new coffee substitute could have waited until the morning."

"Ah, but then I wouldn't have known it wasn't a success, and I'd be drinking that sludge to wake up instead of this," Janeway countered.

Chakotay hesitated. "Look. You know and I know that we've been going nonstop. The last time we visited a planet was hardly an occasion for R-and-R."

Janeway's stomach clenched at the recollection. On Tarakis, the crew had all been forced to relive memories that were not their own. Janeway vividly recalled pleading with Saavedra not to massacre the colonists, but to no avail. Some nights, she still had dreams about it.

"No," she agreed softly, feeling a vestige of the pain brush past her. "It wasn't."

"Astrometrics to Captain Janeway."

"Go ahead, Seven."

"I suggest that you report to astrometrics immediately. And Commander Chakotay as well."

They exchanged glances, and as one rose and headed for astrometrics.

Seven's beautiful visage was unreadable. It usually was, but the request didn't bode well. "What have you got for me, Seven?" asked Janeway.

Quickly the former Borg stepped to her station and deftly manipulated the controls. A star chart appeared on the large screen.

"This," she said. It was all she needed to say.

Janeway's heart, which had lifted a little after the banter she'd exchanged with Chakotay, sank again. She was looking at a star chart that might have been drawn by an artist with an overactive imagination and a bent for the depressing. There wasn't a single asteroid belt, but a whopping *four* of them. Over there—and, now that she looked closer, over there and there too—was evidence of a singularity. A swirl marked the site of what she was afraid was the event horizon of a black hole. There were two red giants. Ripples indicated the presence nearly everywhere of gravity waves.

"I do hope you're not going to tell me that we have to travel through there," Janeway said.

"Unfortunately, the path we need to take in order to stay on course is this." Seven touched a control, and a jagged red line appeared. It went straight through the worst areas. "We could adjust it like so," Seven continued, and plotted an alternative course. "But that would take three weeks longer."

"And a course to avoid this No Man's Land altogether?"

Seven frowned at the unfamiliar term, but replied, "Seventeen months, six weeks, four days, and nine hours. I explored all the various options before calling you, Captain."

"Efficient," said Janeway dryly.

Seven inclined her blond head. "Thank you. I strive to be."

Slowly, Janeway shook her head as her gaze traveled over the charts. She was not about to add seventeen months to their journey. Even if they took the middle option Seven had outlined, the one that missed the worst of it, they were going to be in for a very rough few weeks.

With an odd twinkle in his eye, Chakotay said in a serious voice, "I hate to say it, but it doesn't look good. It doesn't look good at all."

And no doubt Seven was left wondering if she would ever understand non-assimilated humans when Janeway, unable to help herself, burst into laughter.

"We're calling it No Man's Land," said Janeway as the star chart bristling with obstacles appeared on the smaller computer monitor in the briefing room.

"That is an incorrect usage of the term," said Seven, surprising Janeway. "I have researched the phrase. It was used during Earth's First World War to describe the ground between two opposing trenches. We are currently facing no adversary. Therefore, there can be no No Man's Land."

"But we are facing an adversary, Seven," Janeway corrected her gently. "It's the same enemy that we've been locked in battle with ever since the Caretaker snatched us out of our own quadrant. Our adversary is the Delta Quadrant. It's the light-years that lie between us and reaching our loved ones, between our home and us. The No Man's Land of World War I was a bad place to be. It had a great deal of barbed wire, it was full of broken and abandoned military equipment, and after a battle, there were bodies there too. It was hard to gain even a meter of ground of No Man's Land, and that little amount was always dearly bought."

She turned again to regard the ominous star chart,

took in its visible, predictable dangers, and wondered for a brief moment about the dangers they weren't even aware of yet. "No, Seven. I'd say No Man's Land is a perfect way to describe what we're up against."

Seven pursed her full lips in a gesture that Janeway had come to recognize meant she didn't approve, but it didn't matter. No matter what they chose to call this, it was bad news.

"I don't want to head into that space until we're performing at peak ability. Status reports," she requested.

Torres went first. "We're presently performing a level-one diagnostic. Everything seems to be all right. Engineering's ready to tackle it, unless the diagnostic reveals something unexpected."

One by one, they gave their reports. Paris reported that the helm had been performing more than adequately, and added that he had just done something he called a "tune-up" to the *Delta Flyer.* Tuvok was prepared to run a series of drills to make sure tactical was up to par. Harry Kim had nothing to report about ops. The Doctor reported treating only two minor injuries in the last week.

"One of which Mr. Paris incurred in what he describes as a minor disagreement with Seamus in Fair Haven," he added, in a disapproving tone of voice.

"Which won't happen again," Paris insisted a little too vehemently.

Janeway sat for a moment, absorbing the information. She hardly dared believe it, but it seemed as if they were ready to venture forth into No Man's

Land. If that were so, then why did she feel so strangely reluctant?

She had just opened her mouth to order that they proceed first thing in the morning, but Chakotay spoke first.

"There is one thing, Captain."

"What is it, Chakotay?"

"There has been an egregious lack of fun on the part of the captain and the crew," he said in a completely serious voice. "That could have severe repercussions if the crew is not in as good a shape to tackle the challenges of No Man's Land as the ship is."

She raised an eyebrow. "I see. What do you recommend?"

She could tell he was fighting to keep from smiling, but largely succeeding. He rose, went to the screen, and touched it. At once, the image of a planet appeared. It had blue oceans, brown-and-green landmasses, and swirling white clouds. It looked so much like Earth that she felt an unexpected pang of homesickness.

"While Seven of Nine is exemplary in her execution of her duty, she needs to develop a little imagination."

Seven bridled. "I am not accustomed to evaluating situations with regard to—their fun factor."

"My point exactly. This planet is located directly on our way to No Man's Land. It's a perfect class-M. No life, other than plant life, although there are microscopic organisms in the planet's oceans. Someone's many-times-great-grandfather, no doubt, but for the present moment, we won't have to worry about the Prime Directive. There are beaches, mountains, rivers, oceans, rain forests, deserts—you name it. It sounds like an excellent place for shore leave. We could then tackle No Man's Land refreshed and renewed." He looked over at Janeway. "Captain? What do you think?"

Some decisions, Janeway thought, were just easier than others. "Mr. Paris," she said, rising and striving to maintain an authoritarian demeanor, "lay in a direct course for that planet. We could all use some R-and-R."

For once, Chakotay didn't have to do any arm-twisting to get his captain to enjoy a bit of shore leave herself. Janeway was in the second group of people to transport down. Tom Paris, B'Elanna Torres, and Neelix, along with seven others, had already gone on ahead. They had reported that the planet's climate was every bit as nice as Risa's, though, according to Paris, the lack of scores of beautiful women was keenly felt. Janeway wondered if Torres had overheard that last comment, and if so, what her retort might have been.

Ensign Lyssa Campbell, usually a little shy around her captain, positively grinned at Janeway when she came in lugging her paints, palette, and easel.

"Going for a few landscapes?"

Janeway returned the smile. "Absolutely. According to Seven, there are some exquisite mountain ranges. She also went into great detail about how the location I have selected will produce an optimal concentration of particles in the air, resulting in an increased profusion of shorter wavelengths of light."

Lyssa Campbell regarded her blankly. Taking pity on her, Janeway explained, "That's Seven's way of saying the sunsets watched from the beach ought to be particularly colorful."

Campbell blushed. Janeway winked at her and stepped onto the platform. The plan was for her to have several hours of uninterrupted painting time—a rare luxury—before Chakotay transported down with a picnic basket. Janeway knew herself pretty well, and realized that she sometimes didn't take the time she needed to truly relax. Well, Chakotay couldn't call her on it after this.

She was still smiling as she dematerialized.

"The smell of the sea is the same everywhere," said Tom with a sigh of contentment. He and B'Elanna had walked hand in hand by the ocean for about an hour. She had spotted the little cave a short climb up, and now they sat contentedly watching the huge golden sun set over orange and scarlet waves.

"That's poetic license," murmured Torres, who, even though she was arguing with him, still had her eyes closed and was languidly inhaling the afore-mentioned ocean scent. "Every planet has different organisms. Therefore, the smell—"

"Is always enchanting," said Tom. "Just like you."

She opened her eyes and smiled up at him. He reached for her, thinking that this would be a lovely little place for a tryst, when he saw something out of the corner of his eye.

He turned his head and frowned. "There's something out there. In the ocean. Look."

She looked where he pointed. For a moment, he thought his eyes had been playing tricks on him. But then it surfaced again. It was small, dark, and definitely alive.

"But that's not possible," said Torres. "This planet doesn't have any life more developed than amoebas."

"That's definitely a life-form more advanced than an amoeba," said Tom, scrambling to his feet. "And it looks like it's drowning."

CHAPTER
2

DRIVEN BY A POTENT COMBINATION OF URGENCY AND
curiosity, Paris and Torres hastened down the rock
face as quickly as possible. Tom tried to keep one eye
on the struggling creature in the water. They were
close enough now to see that it wasn't a humanoid,
but that didn't slow him down one bit. Paris had a
tremendous fondness for both animals and children, as
long as he wasn't responsible for either for any great
length of time. The thought of some innocent animal
drowning before he could get to it spurred him on.

"Do you see it?" The anxious cry came from
Neelix, who had been wandering barefoot along the
shore looking for interesting rocks. He had been
looking forward to collecting seashells until Paris
had gently reminded him that if there were no life-
forms, there would be no shells of life-forms on the

beach. Now the Talaxian raced with surprising speed toward the spot where the creature was likely to come ashore.

If it came ashore. Even as Tom watched, the creature went down again.

"Dammit," he swore, and jumped the rest of the way to land heavily on the soft, powdery sand. He and Neelix hit the water at the same time, with B'Elanna only a stride behind them.

Tom struck out for the creature. The water was incredibly clear and he could see it now. It was about half a meter long, its thick, dark fur floating about it like wings or tendrils. Other than the languid movement of its fur, it was motionless and was starting to sink toward the bottom. He took a deep breath and dove for it, kicking as hard as he could. His arms closed about it and he struck out for the surface.

"Keep its head above the water," he gasped to Torres, who immediately obliged. Neelix had almost reached them, but now he turned and headed back to the shore. He had been so agitated that he hadn't even taken off the jacket of his heavy, colorful suit. Tom was grateful that he and Torres, anticipating a day at the beach, had opted for more traditional swimwear.

With one arm around the animal *(God, is it still alive? Please let it be alive)*, he struck out for the beach. It seemed so far away now. The creature in the crook of his arm was still warm, at least, and as Paris's feet dug into sand and he stumbled ashore, he felt the beast twitch. It squirmed vigorously, and Paris let out a short, quick laugh.

The animal leaped from his arm to plop on the sand. There it coughed, vomiting up seawater, and trembled pathetically. It made no attempt to flee. Rather, it looked up quizzically at the three *Voyager* crewmen.

"I've n-notified the captain," said Neelix. He was shivering in his sodden suit. "Sh-she's on her way."

"What is it doing here?" asked Torres, voicing the more pressing question rather than the all-too-common *What is it?* Chances were they'd never really know what it was, but maybe they could determine why it, a developed creature, was on this allegedly uninhabited planet.

Neelix squatted down. "Poor little thing," he said softly. He extended a hand. The creature sniffed at it.

Paris regarded it in more detail. It was small, weighing only a couple of kilos. All that hair, which had weighed it down in the ocean, probably made it look bigger than it was.

"It looks like some kind of canine," he said.

"No big bad wolf, that's for sure," said Torres, joining Neelix in reaching out a hand. The creature sniffed her, its dark purple nose quivering, then extended a black tongue and licked her hand. She laughed, surprised.

"It's either fearless or has been domesticated," said Neelix.

"Step away from it," came Janeway's brisk voice.

"Oh, Captain, it's harmless," said Neelix.

"Not until my tricorder says so," Janeway replied. She was dressed in an outfit Paris had never seen her in: a long shirt and baggy pants. It looked very comfortable and there were lots of colorful splotches of paint on it. And some colorful splotches of paint on his captain as well, but he thought it better not to mention it. So this was Captain Janeway at leisure. It was a good look for her.

She was all business now as she knelt near the animal and scanned it with the tricorder. "Canine," she said. Paris threw Torres a *told-you-so* look. "Carnivore. No signs of disease. Well nourished and completely healthy."

The creature lowered its hindquarters. If it weren't for the orange and red fur, the purple nose, and the slitted eyes, Tom could have sworn it was a dog.

"And friendly," Janeway admitted, breaking into a smile and petting the creature's sodden pelt. "The question is, my friend, what are you doing here, hmm? How is it that you're well nourished on meat when there's nothing here big enough to catch your eye?"

She straightened. Neelix picked up the creature and cuddled it. It ducked its head against his chest, seemingly completely at home in a humanoid's arms.

"This has got to be somebody's pet," stated Paris. He didn't know how he knew, he just did.

"I'm inclined to agree with you, Tom," said Janeway. She tapped her combadge. "Janeway to *Voyager.*"

"I was just about to contact you, Captain," came Chakotay's voice. "We detected a sudden, brief surge of energy. Did you see anything?"

Janeway glanced at the creature in Neelix's arms. It was shivering and, Paris thought, not very happy about being soaked to the bone.

"We did see something, but more on that in a minute. We noticed no surge of energy. Where was it located?"

"Approximately ninety meters northeast from

where the four of—wait a minute, I'm detecting another life sign. It's right on top of Neelix!"

"That was the other thing I was going to tell you about. It's harmless, but it's raising a lot of questions. Tom, Torres, Neelix—any of you see anything?"

Paris felt his face grow warm. Until they'd spotted the dog-alien-thing, he'd been far too engrossed in B'Elanna's warmth and the scent of the sea to have noticed anything short of a Borg cube. "Negative, Captain."

Neelix also looked uncomfortable. He'd probably had his eyes glued to the sand, on the lookout for some interesting rocks. He, too, shook his head.

To his relief, Janeway seemed as annoyed with herself as she was with them. "I was concentrating on mixing cadmium red with thalo blue myself."

"I'm not surprised," said Chakotay. "The energy pulse only registered for a second or two here. It might not even have been visible to the naked eye."

"Captain," said Paris, "we saw the dog drowning in precisely the spot that Chakotay had indicated. This thing couldn't have evolved naturally on this planet. I'm certain that the energy pulse has something to do with why it's here."

Janeway nodded. "I agree with you, Mr. Paris. It could have been a transport of some kind."

"What kind of monster would deliberately transport a little dog into the middle of the ocean?" exclaimed Neelix, cuddling his new friend closer.

"It's not a dog," Janeway said, "and I suggest that you not get too attached to it."

"We're not going to leave it here?" interjected B'Elanna. Tom turned to her, surprised and pleased.

It wasn't like B'Elanna to champion puppies. She looked uncomfortable with the outburst. "I mean, it didn't evolve here. It couldn't survive."

"Yeah," put in Tom helpfully.

"Look at this little face, Captain," urged Neelix, lifting the animal to within inches of Janeway's nose. "He'll die if we abandon him. He'll starve to death—a slow, agonizing, heartless, cruel—"

Janeway lifted a hand in surrender. "All right, you've made your point. What I want to know is what created that energy pulse. If we can find who did it, then maybe we could figure out who this fellow belongs to and—"

Paris's blue eyes widened. They had all turned to face the spot where Chakotay had told them the pulse had manifested. Right before their eyes, a thin, horizontal line appeared from nowhere. It grew in length, then shunted downward at a right angle until there was a large rectangle extending into the sea. It was as if someone had taken a knife and carved the sky like a jack-o'-lantern, revealing only darkness beyond.

The dog-thing wriggled in Neelix's arms and let out a sharp, loud sound that reminded Paris of a bark.

"It—it looks like a doorway," said Torres, her voice quavering only slightly.

"Yes," breathed Janeway, "but a doorway to where?"

Shore leave was abruptly terminated. Janeway, who moments before had been utterly absorbed in her painting, could barely spare the time to put the caps on the tubes of paint before she hastily ordered them, along with herself, directly transported to her quarters. She dressed quickly, groaning a little as she realized she'd gotten paint in her hair, and quickly scrubbed it out. Her mind was racing a thousand kilometers a minute.

The bridge was monitoring the strange door. It was reportedly stable, for the moment. The energy spike had been like nothing they'd ever seen before. Chakotay's voice wafted to her ears through her combadge, penetrating her thoughts.

"Our sensors can't penetrate inside," he was saying as Janeway brushed at her damp hair.

"I want a closer look at it."

A sigh. "I was afraid you'd say that. We can maneuver a probe down—"

"No. I want to see it for myself."

"That could be dangerous."

"Understood. We'll take a probe with us. And if it's safe, I want to go through."

A heavy, laden pause. "Captain?"

"Chakotay, it's the only conceivable way the dog could have gotten on that planet. If it's safe enough for the dog, it's safe enough for us."

"So you're calling it a dog now too."

Briefly, Janeway glanced over at the holophoto of her beloved Molly and her once-beloved Mark. There was still a pang when she looked at this image of them, captured forever in time, when Molly was young, Janeway was home, and Mark was desperately in love with her. As she had been with him.

It was Molly she was looking at now, though, not Mark. She recalled finding her at a pound on Taurus Ceti IV, saw again the pup's lively enthusiasm, her spunk, her spirit. There hadn't been room in her life for a dog at the time, but she'd made room.

Surprising herself, Janeway blinked back tears at the memory of housetraining the puppy, of watching her ungainly ambling wobble mature into the sleek, graceful gait of a purebred Irish setter. Molly was beautiful, calm, obedient, and loving. She had so wanted to be present at the birth of Molly's puppies. Molly would be growing older by this point. Were there white hairs on that long muzzle? Stiffness in the liquid joints? Even her puppies would be well into their adult years. Time was harsher on some than others. Janeway forgave herself for the quick rush of tears, gone as soon as they had arrived.

And now this little bundle, which was currently quarantined in sickbay, had appeared on the proverbial doorstep. Was it so wrong to call it a dog? It was of a similar species, had clearly been domesticated, and had a nature as sweet as Neelix's. Which was actually saying a hell of a lot.

"Yes," she stated. "I'm calling it a dog." Her curiosity was aroused by the creature and the mysterious doorway through which it had likely arrived. "Have Lieutenant Paris prepare the *Delta Flyer* and fetch our little friend from sickbay. We're going back down."

Paris met her in the docking bay a few moments later, carrying the "dog" and a crate in which to contain it once they boarded the shuttlecraft. It looked much happier and considerably drier than when Janeway had seen it about a half hour ago. Its fur was clean and dried and fluffed in a fashion that practically begged for her to run her fingers through it. She obliged, and found the creature absolutely silky to the touch. It looked at her and blinked its slitted eyes.

"Think he likes you, Captain."

She smiled at Tom. "Perceptive animal. Come on." She climbed into the *Flyer.* Paris emulated her. Janeway alternately coaxed and shoved the animal into the crate, then stowed it in the back. It whimpered a little, but stayed put. Janeway moved up to the front and took the seat behind Paris, letting him do what he was best at—piloting.

The doors opened, and the *Delta Flyer* took off into open space. The two were silent as they made their way to the planet. Finally Paris spoke up. "Too bad everyone couldn't have had some shore leave."

"We do seem to keep running into adventures, don't we?" his captain replied, her eyes on the readings. "I don't know about you, but much as I enjoy R-and-R, nothing gets my blood going like a good, old-fashioned, scientific mystery. And we've got a fine example right here."

They entered the planet's atmosphere and Tom checked the coordinates. Smoothly, the *Flyer* made its way through white clouds. Below them stretched the ocean, blue-green and beautiful and devoid of life large enough to see. Janeway couldn't help but wonder what creatures would eventually develop here in this fertile, friendly world.

With a couple of taps of his fingers, Paris brought the small vessel down low. It almost skimmed the surface of the waves. Janeway wondered if Paris was doing this to impress her with his skill. It wasn't necessary; she knew he was the best. That's why she'd asked him to join her, all those years ago back in New Zealand.

It was just barely visible up ahead now, the strange portal. Janeway sat up straighter, her heart starting to beat faster. Paris slowed; then they came to a stop. Gently, Paris maneuvered the *Flyer* into the water and the small vessel began to rock with the motion of the waves.

The doors hissed open and Janeway stood, lightly touching the back of the chair to keep her balance. Paris was very good indeed; he'd brought them to within a meter of the door itself. She went to the doors and got as close as she could to the strange portal.

Janeway peered inside. Nothing. The blackness was absolute. She tapped her combadge. "Janeway to *Voyager*."

"Go ahead, Captain," said Tuvok.

"We are activating the probe and are just about to send it through." As she spoke, she extended a hand. Paris, who had risen to stand beside her, placed the small orb in her palm. She thumbed it and it came to life. Small blue and green lights flickered on its metallic surface. Gently, Janeway tossed it in the direction of the doorway. The momentum propelled it forward, humming.

Janeway held her breath.

It was within a third of a meter of the doorway—a few centimeters—

—inside—

Then it was gone. It vanished as if it had never been.

"We have lost all traces of the probe," came Tuvok's calm voice, filled with none of the disappointment that was flooding Janeway's mind.

"So have we. It disappeared." She closed her eyes and sighed heavily. "Looks like we have a new passenger. Tom, take us back."

He stared at her. "That's it?"

She regarded him coolly. "I can't see anything. Our sensors can't detect anything. There are no lives at stake here. The probe is utterly gone. I'm not about to send that animal through there without being certain it's safe. And I'm certainly not going to order any of my crew through there for no good reason. Do you understand, Mr. Paris?"

He averted his gaze. "Yes, ma'am," he said, and entered the controls.

As she sank back in her chair, Janeway regretted the harsh tone of voice she'd used with him. In truth, she was angry herself, at being cheated of an adventure. She'd have loved to go through, see what was on the other side, but there was no way to justify the risk. Her crew came first. Her scientific curiosity would just have to go unappeased today.

And in the meantime, *Voyager* now had a mascot.

She forced herself not to turn back and look with disappointed longing as the portal vanished into the distance.

CHAPTER

3

"WONDER IF HE'S HOUSEBROKEN," TOM MUSED, TO break the awkward silence as the *Delta Flyer* headed back to rendezvous with *Voyager.*

"If not, it's a good opportunity for you to take some responsibility," Janeway replied, recognizing Paris's overture for what it was and more than willing to put the tense, disappointing moment behind them.

"Me?" Paris turned his head in her direction so quickly she thought he'd given himself whiplash. "Oh, no."

The as of yet unnamed "dog," freed from the crate and perhaps sensing that it was the topic of conversation, ambled forward. Janeway picked it up and placed it in her lap. "You rescued him, Tom," said Janeway, scratching the animal behind what ap-

24

peared to be ears. "Yes he did, didn't he?" she crooned.

The animal licked her face.

"Well, yeah, but that was a humanitarian gesture. Neelix would make a much better owner than I would."

Janeway thought of how protective Neelix had been of the creature. Small, lost things seemed to gravitate to him, didn't they?

"We'll see if Neelix is willing. As long as one of you steps up to take responsibility, I don't care who."

"Thought maybe you might want him," ventured Paris.

Janeway shook her head. "No. I already have a dog. Several, in fact. This one needs someone else." Again she scratched the animal, enjoying the incredible silky feel of his fur against her finger. "What shall we call you, little fellow?"

"Chakotay to Janeway."

"Go ahead, Commander."

"Sorry the door mystery didn't get solved, but we've got a new one for you to tackle once you come aboard."

"I can't wait."

"What have you got, Commander?" asked Janeway, stepping briskly from the turbolift onto the bridge.

"Spatial dislocation energy readings," Chakotay replied, rising from the command chair and yielding it to his captain. "Similar to what we saw on the planet, but much more intense."

Janeway sat down and called up her viewscreen and regarded the readings. "Opinions?"

"We can't get very good readings on it," said Chakotay. "It could be another door. But as you can see, the readings are slightly different and much stronger."

Once again, Janeway felt the yearning to step through that door, felt the pang of having had to deny that yearning. She was a rationalist, not a dreamer, but she had felt pulled to that door. Choosing not to step through had been one of the hardest things she'd ever done. And now here was something very close to that, cropping up again.

"This can't be a coincidence," she said to herself. "It's too close."

"It's a considerable distance out of our way," said Chakotay, "but it is a fascinating phenomenon. And we are explorers, so . . ."

He didn't need to complete the sentence. "Agreed. Let's explore. Mr. Paris," she said to Tom, who had just entered after having dropped off the unnamed animal with Neelix, "you won't have time to warm that seat, I'm afraid. You and Seven take the *Delta Flyer* and investigate. Let us know what you think."

Paris raised an eyebrow and spun around on his heels.

"Who's keeping the dog?" asked Chakotay.

"Not sure yet," said Janeway, "but I'm betting on Neelix."

"Wish we could have gone through," said Paris to Seven as they settled back in their chairs. It was going to take about an hour to reach their destination. Paris stretched.

"Explain." Seven's eyes were on the screen, flicking back and forth between the computer's graphic display and a staggering line of equations.

"The doorway. On the planet. Captain wouldn't let us go through."

"A logical decision."

"Yeah, but still. It would have been exciting."

She turned her cool blue gaze on him for a moment. "Excitement is irrelevant."

Paris shook his head. "At least we got the dog."

"Pets are also irrelevant. Especially aboard a starship."

"Bet the kids will love him."

Seven's full lips curved in a slight frown. "I am certain that the Borg children will also find this pet irrelevant."

Tom thought of the cute little fellow licking Janeway's face. "Don't be too sure."

She turned to him and accused, "You are making conversation about inane matters. We should be focusing our attention on the task at hand. Surely that would be . . . exciting."

Paris glanced over at the dizzying list of equations. "Hoo boy, more fun than a barrel of monkeys."

Seven did not even bother to ask him to explain that one. With thinly concealed exasperation, she returned to her task.

Paris sighed and adjusted the controls from autopilot to manual. At least it would give him something to do. Seven was gorgeous. Seven was brilliant. Seven was efficient and accurate and meticulous and logical and all those other precise and annoying adjectives she liked to use. But when you came right down to it, when you were stuck with her in a shuttle for an hour, Seven wasn't much fun.

All of a sudden, Tom frowned at the readings. Something was happening.

"Captain," said Tuvok. "I think you should see this."

Janeway activated her screen. "My God," she whispered. "Will you look at that."

The computer graphics had marked the spatial distortion with a yellow, pulsating circle. Before her eyes, the shimmering image expanded, then contracted back to its original size. All around it, small pinpricks of yellow appeared, each one pulsing and growing until they were all the same size as the original distortion.

Janeway met Chakotay's dark gaze. "There are more of them," she said.

"Many more," said Chakotay.

"Onscreen," Janeway ordered.

On the massive screen that was *Voyager*'s major window on the cosmos, Tuvok had placed the graphic display. They weren't looking at the actual distortions, but a computer representation.

"I am placing the original distortion in the exact center of the screen," said Tuvok.

As they watched, one by one, blips appeared, grew, and steadied. At first there were only five or six, but within a minute, there were dozens.

At that moment, she heard Tom Paris's voice.

"Delta Flyer to Voyager."

"We're reading you, Tom," his captain replied. "From here it looks like that single distortion isn't alone anymore."

"We're monitoring the situation," Paris answered.

"Captain—other lost puppies are following us home. Can we keep them?"

Janeway smiled her warmest smile as the two aliens transported aboard her ship. Tom had warned her that they were frightened, but probably harmless. They'd had some incredible story, which Seven had declined to relate, indicating that it would be best if Janeway heard them out herself.

Her first impression seemed to confirm that of Paris. The two humanoids who materialized on the ship literally clung to each other and looked around with wide eyes.

They were tall, about two and a half meters, and quite powerfully built. Small, iridescent scales covered what flesh was visible, but they had long black hair and the female had breasts, indicating that they were mammalian. Their hands had long, tapered fingers and a peculiar hornlike growth protruding from the wrists. Slightly elongated mouths reminded her of muzzles, and they had vestigial, stumpy tails. Janeway was immediately reminded of the Cardassians, but there was nothing of that species' trademark arrogance about these two, a male and a female. They clutched each other's hands and their red, double-pupiled eyes were wide. Their breath came quickly.

"Welcome aboard my ship," Janeway said as pleasantly as possible. "My lieutenant tells me that you're lost, just as we are."

As she had hoped, that got their attention. The female cocked her head. "You are lost?"

"Yes, we are. But we're trying to get home. We hope to assist you in that quest too. Are you hungry?"

They glanced at each other. Finally, as if it was a source of great shame, the male admitted, "Our food and water supplies ran out several days ago."

"Then I should take you to sickbay at once," stated Janeway. "We'll make sure that you're in good health, and then we'll have lunch together."

The female looked frightened. "Your . . . doctor," she said hesitantly. "He does not perform . . . experiments?"

Good Lord, no wonder these people were frightened. Seven and Tom had to have done a bang-up job to simply convince them to come aboard *Voyager*. She stepped forward impulsively, compassion warring with righteous anger.

"No one aboard this ship will harm you in any way," she stated. "You are guests here, not captives. You can return to your vessel any time you wish. We'd like to help you."

"Why?" asked the male.

"Because it's the right thing to do. People have helped us in our search to get home. It's the least we can do to help others in a similar situation. I would like you to see our doctor because if you are suffering from malnutrition or dehydration or any other ailment, he can treat it. If you don't want to see him, I won't force you."

They exchanged glances again. Finally, the male nodded. "I am Torar. This is my mate, Ara. Our people are called the Nenlar."

"It's a pleasure to meet you. Come. Let's go to sickbay and see what the Doctor has to say. Then I'll be happy to see what we can do to help you."

Janeway tried to observe unobtrusively as the

three of them made their way to sickbay. Not only were they exhausted and famished, but there was a constant air of apprehension about the two Nenlars. They started at every unfamiliar noise, twisted their heads to follow each person who passed them in the corridors. By the time they reached sickbay, the two of them and, to some extent, their host as well, were nervous wrecks.

Janeway smiled as she caught sight of the little dog, still ensconced in one of the smaller observation areas. It immediately rose to its feet upon sight of her and began barking.

The Doctor frowned. "According to Mr. Neelix, he wants to play."

"I'm sure he does," said Janeway, smiling and placing her hand on the clear partition. The dog wriggled ecstatically. "When will you let him?"

"Mr. Neelix is planning to drop by a little later with the children for a play session. We'll see how the animal interacts with them. If he can be trusted, I'll relinquish him into Mr. Neelix's capable hands. In the meantime, I see you've brought me some other patients." He turned a beaming countenance upon the Nenlars.

Ara's eyes had widened so large they threatened to fall out of her skull. At once, Janeway made the connection they had and hastened to reassure her guests. "This is a lower species," she said, indicating the dog. "We believe it is a domesticated animal of some sort. You won't be placed in a holding area."

Ara visibly relaxed, and Torar smiled shakily. "Of course not," he said with false heartiness, as if he had never had any doubt.

For all his arrogance, the Doctor was a perceptive hologram, and his bedside manner had been steadily improving since his original activation so many years ago. "Please have a seat on one of the beds," he invited his guests.

They complied immediately, both on the same bed, which Janeway suspected was not what the Doctor had intended. Nonetheless, he began to examine Ara.

Janeway took the opportunity to try to engage them in conversation. "Lieutenant Paris says that you told him and Seven that you were lost. What happened? Where is your homeworld?"

It ought to have been an easy, straightforward question. But the Nenlars again exchanged glances. Finally, Torar spoke.

"We know what happened, but we do not understand it. And we cannot tell you where our world is, because we haven't the slightest idea where we are at present."

"Go on," Janeway urged.

Again, the hesitation, the looks. It was beginning to set off Janeway's warning bells, but she would listen first before making judgments.

"Our planet was . . . severely damaged in a war many centuries ago. 'Devastated' would not be too harsh a word." There was a hint of anger in Torar's voice even now. "It was a long, painful path to recovery, but we are a determined people and we finally again discovered a way to reach the stars. We used faster-than-light travel to search for ways to enrich our world—new crops, new technology, new ideas. Many intrepid souls left our homeworld altogether, to scratch out new lives for themselves elsewhere. We like to observe first, then make first contact on our own terms, once we determine a species is not a threat. We have . . . an ingrained fear of being dominated, taken advantage of, again. You can imagine, Captain Janeway, how unsettling it was when we had no idea where in the universe our little scout ship was."

Janeway nodded in sympathy. The Doctor had finished with his preliminary examination of Ara and turned his attention to Torar. The sudden move of the tricorder in his direction caused Torar to flinch, albeit briefly.

He recovered quickly and continued. "When the portal appeared, it did not seem too dangerous to venture through it."

"Portal?" exclaimed Janeway, fully alert now. "Describe it."

"It was like a strange doorway in space," said Ara. "Big enough for our ship to traverse. We thought we could venture through, see what was on the other side, and return safely." She hesitated. "We were terribly wrong."

Janeway's skin prickled. She'd been right not to go through that doorway with Paris and the dog. Although it had felt so very wrong at the time. . . .

"The moment we had passed through, the portal vanished. We couldn't see it; our ship sensors couldn't detect it. When another one opened up shortly afterward, we foolishly thought it was the same portal."

"But it wasn't," said Janeway softly.

"No," said Torar. "It led to an entirely different place. Nothing was the same. No recognizable stars, nothing. More and more portals opened up. We began to grow frightened."

"Fear," said Ara, "is also ingrained in us. You cannot imagine the discipline required to subdue it."

From what they had said about their race being terrorized, Janeway suspected she could. She made a mental note to have Tuvok talk to these people. Who knew but that he might be able to teach them some mental disciplines to handle this deep-set, racial terror.

"We panicked," said Torar, hanging his head in shame. "We went through every portal that appeared."

"There were dozens," said Ara swiftly.

"Hundreds. We lost count of how many we tried, hoping each one would be the one that led back to our sector."

"None of them was."

"Some of them opened into what we think were other dimensions," said Torar. At once, Janeway thought of fluidic space. She wondered if they had encountered Species 8472. "It was terrifying, Captain. Terrifying. When finally we ended up here—wherever here may be—we realized that, no matter where we were, we were in normal space again. We calmed down somewhat and refused to be tempted by any other portals that manifested."

"A very wise choice," said the Doctor.

"I agree," said Janeway. "And you've been wandering this sector since?"

"Yes," said Ara. "With portals opening all the time, taunting us. But we didn't yield, not even when our supplies ran out." She lowered her eyes and spoke softly. "There are things that are more frightening than the thought of starving to death with one's mate, Captain. And we saw some of those things."

Spontaneously, Janeway reached out a hand and placed it on Ara's. The Nenlar tensed, but after a long moment, her slender fingers opened and curled around Janeway's, accepting the other woman's sympathy. Janeway squeezed gently, and then released Ara's hand.

"With your permission, I'd like to send a team over to start effecting repairs and resupplying your vessel," she said.

This time, there was no hesitation. "You are kind, Captain," Torar answered at once. "We are grateful for any help you choose to give us."

Janeway was pleased. She'd won their trust. "Doctor, what's the diagnosis?" she asked.

"From what I can determine, never having encountered this species before," said the Doctor, "the two seem in fairly good health, considering all they've undergone. I'd like to rehydrate them and give them some nutritional supplements before releasing them to Mr. Neelix for a hearty lunch."

The two nodded. Quickly the Doctor applied a series of hyposprays. Gingerly, the two touched their necks after he was done, but they already looked better, more alert.

Janeway touched her combadge. "Torres, this is Janeway. Can you prepare a team to transport over to the Nenlar vessel? I'd like to start repairs as soon as possible."

"Aye, Captain," Torres replied.

"Come. We'll get you some lunch."

* * *

The lunch, while not one of Neelix's better repasts, was devoured hungrily by the Nenlars. They did not seem familiar with eating utensils and used their long, clever fingers to place food into their mouths. Nonetheless, not a crumb was dropped and the entire process was as formal and tidy as many a Starfleet banquet Janeway had been forced to attend. Manners came in all shapes and sizes, and Janeway was not about to pass judgment. They did notice the crew eating with utensils, and Janeway suspected that they'd get around to asking about such strange and unnecessary implements later.

She learned a little more about them as she ate her own lunch, which was a ham and Swiss on rye. She had decided at the last minute to forgo Neelix's *yruss*-and-broccoli (by all accounts one of his tastier dishes) and eat something that she normally ate with her hands, to make her guests feel more at ease. They were shy, peaceful, and cautious. Ara and Torar revealed that they were actually considered quite the brave souls on their planet, for daring to embark on dangerous space missions to explore the sector in search of technologies to bring back to benefit their world.

It wasn't until dessert, however, that Janeway learned the name of the race that had so traumatized the Nenlar centuries earlier. Clutching a warm, just-replicated chocolate chip cookie in one hand and a large glass of milk in the other, Ara reminded Janeway of a frightened child as she spoke.

"Iudka," she said, as if uttering the worst word in the universe. And by her standards, of course, she was. "They came and plundered our world. They took everything that was of any value on the surface and in the oceans, and ripped open the ground to take more. When they were done, they bombed every major city to ashes, then left to do the same to other innocent worlds. We were not even capable of spaceflight at that time. It took us centuries to recover, centuries more to dare to venture into the skies, the same place from whence our tormentors had come. But we did so." She lifted her head and her eyes gleamed with pride. No longer did she look like a terrified girl, but like a warrior. "We were brave."

You were indeed, thought Janeway, wondering whether, if the same thing had happened in Earth's nineteenth century, her own people would have had that same courage.

She left them in Neelix's care, and he promised to show them around the ship.

The rest of the day unfolded as usual. With Ara and Torar's permission, Torres's team had downloaded the contents of the Nenlar ship's computer. All the information it contained would be fed into *Voyager*'s computer. With a little bit of luck, it would yield some clue about the Nenlars' place of origin, and a way to get them back.

Janeway was in the midst of a dream in which Molly was a puppy again, wagging her red tail and chewing happily on a rubber bone, when the crisp voice of the computer startled her awake.

"What . . . oh." She sat up and knuckled sleep out of her eyes. "Repeat message, computer."

"Download and examination of the contents of the Nenlar vessel computer is complete."

Fully alert now, Janeway asked, "Can you determine the location of the Nenlar homeworld?"

"Affirmative. The Nenlar homeworld is the fourth planet from the central star in the Alungis system, located in Sector 48472, in the Beta Quadrant."

CHAPTER

4

WHEN JANEWAY BROKE THE NEWS A FEW HOURS LATER in a senior officer staff meeting, everyone started talking at once.

"Beta Quadrant? Are they near Qo'noS?"

"Could we retrace the various portals?"

"Are they stable?"

Janeway raised her hands for silence. "Their world is nowhere near the Klingon Empire, even with their documentation there is no way to retrace the precise number of portals the Nenlars went through, and the portals themselves are quite far from stable. I entertained those thoughts myself, but the final outcome of all of this is, the Nenlars are almost as far from home as we are, and have about as much likelihood of getting back as we do."

She surveyed her senior officers, and then her eyes

came to rest on the two Nenlars sitting beside her. "I'm sorry," she said gently. "What we can do, is—"

"Kim to Janeway."

Kim was manning the bridge. Janeway frowned. "Go ahead, Mr. Kim."

"It seems that the Nenlars weren't the only ones who got tricked by all those portals. I'm picking up readings of more portals opening and several ships entering this sector through them."

"Stations," said Janeway. The meeting could wait. There was no telling if the crews of all those ships appearing out of nowhere would be as friendly as the Nenlars.

She strode onto the bridge and looked at the viewscreen. "You weren't exaggerating, Mr. Kim," she said softly, with a bit of awe.

Before her was an amazing spectacle. The background of space and stars was now being decorated with mysterious portals, some opening and closing almost immediately, others opening and remaining so. Moving about and sometimes through these gateways was an amazing variety of ships.

"Mr. Kim, prepare to send an open message."

"Go ahead, Captain."

"This is Captain Kathryn Janeway of the Federation starship *Voyager* to all ships in the immediate vicinity. It is likely that you have all recently traveled through some kind of portal in space." Even as she spoke, three more doorways in space opened. Three more ships zipped out. This was madness. What the hell was going on? This made no sense. If the portals were accidental, then the odds of them opening like this were astronomical. If they weren't, if someone had created them, it wasn't logical to have so many opening all at once in the same place. She shook her head, dismissing any rational argument, and merely chose to accept what was.

"While I cannot speak for all of you, I can speak for myself and my ship. We have no hostile intentions toward any of you. Please do not traverse any of the gateways unless you are certain of where they will open. There is an excellent chance that if you do so, you will become more lost than you already are. We are open for your response."

The minute she'd uttered the words, poor Harry Kim was bombarded by replies. It sounded like gibberish as the Universal Translator frantically tried to compensate.

"One at a time, Mr. Kim," Janeway said.

"Aye, Captain," replied Kim distractedly, his fingers flying. "Here we go, in no particular order."

"This is Leader Sinimar Arkathi, of the Todanian vessel the *Relka*. We demand to know why you have brought us here."

"Greetings, Captain Janeway. I am Commander Ellia, of the Salamar vessel the *Umul*. Do you perhaps have a map of these vexing portals we could negotiate for?"

"He-hello? We're the Kuluuk. Please don't hurt us. Who are you, please? Did you bring us here?"

"Captain Janeway. I give you respectful greetings, in the honored conventions of my people. By our custom, here are the names of every crew member aboard my vessel, beginning with mine. I am Ophar, daughter of Willar, son of . . ."

And on and on they came, a dizzying array of

names and lists of species and vessels. Every one of them had a different tone in responding to Janeway's original hail. Janeway threw Chakotay a look of amused exasperation, which he returned with a knowing grin.

Until one name stopped her cold.

"This is Commander Kelmar, of the Iudka vessel the *Nivvika*. We would appreciate any information you have on these portals."

Iudka. The race that had almost wiped out the Nenlar.

Torar and Ara had been standing behind her and she heard them inhale swiftly. Craning her neck to look at them, Janeway said, "Don't worry. I won't let them hurt you."

More titles, pleas, accusations. More species that they'd never heard of. And finally, one that they had. For the second time in five minutes, Janeway's heart sped up with apprehension.

"We have heard of you, *Voyager*. I am Alpha, commander of the Hirogen vessel the *Rhev*."

Finally, after almost two hours, the manifestation of the portals and the ships they disgorged slowed and eventually stopped. Attempting to contact them all individually during this time would have been an exercise in futility. Janeway had to wait until the immense flow had slowed to a trickle. Now she sent out a second message.

"This is Captain Janeway, again to all vessels in the area. We have heard from sixty-two different vessels, representing a total of forty-eight different races. Some of you have sought aid, while others of you have threatened aggression. I understand your confusion; we are confused ourselves as to the nature and purpose, if any, of this phenomenon. With so many individuals involved, it would be useless to try to conduct any meaningful exchange via viewscreens. I propose the following: Each vessel sends a single representative to my ship, *Voyager.* We hold a meeting. Share information. Perhaps one of us has a clue that the others do not. We are all lost here, some to a greater extent than the others. There would be no purpose in hostilities at this juncture for any of us. Our facilities can accommodate the number in comfort. Our translation and transportation devices are more than adequate for what is required."

She paused, and then continued. "I understand what a leap of faith it will be to some of you to transport blindly to my vessel with nothing but my word that you will be safe. To those of you who do not wish to attend, I understand. You won't be forced to come. But you may lose your only chance to return to your own system. You have twenty of our minutes to consider the offer, and then I would appreciate hearing from every vessel. Janeway out."

"Captain, you can't invite the Iudka aboard!" cried Torar.

She turned to look at him. "I can't not invite their commander and have an open house for the other sixty-one captains," she said mildly. "Please don't worry. I will tolerate no violence aboard this vessel. You have my word that you will come to no harm."

"But—"

Janeway held up a hand. "It's my understanding

that the repairs are nearly complete aboard your ship, Torar. If you like, we will replenish your supplies and you may leave immediately."

"And go where?" Torar cried.

"My point exactly. When was the last time you encountered the Iudka?"

Ara looked uncomfortable. "There has been no formal contact for over two hundred years," she admitted. "We have heard rumors, but we had hoped they had died out."

Janeway chose to overlook the vitriol. It wasn't her place to judge. But she was not about to have this parliament of aliens hamstrung by centuries-old fears. "You have changed a great deal since the Iudka last saw you. Perhaps they have as well."

"Evil does not gentle into goodness," spat Torar.

"But *people* can and do change," Janeway replied. "If you don't want to give them the benefit of the doubt, that's your decision. I won't force you to attend this conference. But I won't let your worries do anything to hamper this opportunity for a meeting of minds. Now. Do you wish to attend this gathering?"

No answer at first; then Torar said, "May we sit as far away from the Iudka as possible?"

"Of course," said Janeway, relieved that they were even coming at all.

The Nenlars returned to their vessel to prepare. Janeway sent a final announcement to the assembled races, specifying the place and time at which the meeting would occur.

She fussed with her hair at the mirror, pausing for a moment to regard herself. She had to admit, she looked good in her dress uniform. Janeway had decided to wear it—and require it of all her officers who would also be attending—to emphasize the importance of the meeting and to make it as formal as possible. With so many divergent species in attendance, there were bound to be some bruised egos and perhaps downright outbursts. By announcing at the outset that this was a formal negotiation among equals, and treating the meeting with that level of respect, she hoped to nip any problems in the bud. These people who would shortly be boarding her vessel might not be ambassadors in an official sense, but there would likely be a record number of First Contacts made here today.

The chime at her door startled her out of her reverie. "Come," she called.

Chakotay entered, looking strikingly handsome in his dress uniform. "Status?" she asked, turning to face him.

"Cargo Bay One is presently masquerading as a Federation ceremony hall," he told her.

"I hope it can carry off the illusion," she replied as together they strode into the corridor. "Did all the representatives submit their requirements?"

"Most of them. I've never seen such an interesting assembly of seating arrangements in my life. Those who can't adapt to our atmosphere will be linked via viewscreens. Fortunately, it's a relatively small number. Some of them have already started arriving."

"I hate it when your guests are early," Janeway said. They entered the turbolift. "Cargo Bay One."

"Neelix is doing an admirable job of hosting in your absence," Chakotay assured her.

"Is he serving food?" The possibilities of inadvertently causing offense with the wrong kind of comestibles was staggering.

"He's done his homework," Chakotay said. "And it's all replicated food."

"Thank God for small favors," Janeway said. The turbolift came to a halt.

He put a hand on her arm. "Kathryn," he said quietly, "do you have any plan of action here I should know about?"

"Not a damn thing," she replied gaily as they approached the cargo bay. "I'm playing this all by ear." She squared her shoulders. "Well, here goes nothing."

The door hissed open and Janeway noticed two things immediately. One, there was an incredible volume of conversation, some of it angry-sounding. Two, there were an amazing number of bodies crammed into the cargo bay, and *everyone* seemed to be moving quickly, shoving past his neighbor.

As swift and silent as a cat, Tuvok appeared beside her out of nowhere. She didn't even have to ask for a status update before he spoke.

"This is a highly agitated crowd, Captain. They have not yet demonstrated any physical violence, however. I have twenty-five security personnel distributed throughout the room, some of them clothed so as to blend in with the crowd. All are armed with phasers on stun. We are prepared to erect forcefields if necessary, and—"

She raised a hand to stop him. "I'm sure you've got everything completely under control, Tuvok," she said with a calmness she didn't fully feel. *Showtime,* she thought.

"Could everyone please take a seat?" No response. "Computer, adjust volume of my voice through the translator."

"Volume adjusted."

"Could everyone please take a seat?" Janeway's voice was incredibly loud, and had the desired result. All conversation ceased, and all heads turned to look at her. She felt a flutter of butterflies in her stomach and forced a smile. "I'm sure we'd all like to get this started," she said. "It will be easier if everyone is seated."

More milling about, but this time, Janeway was relieved to see, to an ultimate purpose. All the aliens assembled whose anatomy permitted them to sit did so. Janeway didn't know which ones were the Iudka, but she spotted the Nenlars huddled together against a far wall and guessed that the Iudka were in the place farthest from them. She looked in that direction. Nobody there looked like the monsters the Nenlars had described. But then again, they probably wouldn't.

She strode forward with a confidence she did not really feel to the podium at the front of the hastily redecorated cargo bay.

"First, let me thank you all for coming. I can only imagine how you are all feeling. It took a leap of faith for you to attend without knowing what other races might be here, and I commend you for that courage.

"You have all received information on my vessel, *Voyager,* and know that we, like you, ended up here in what we know as the Delta Quadrant by accident. We have spent over five years searching for a way home, but also putting to good use the unique opportunity that being here has presented us."

She scanned the crowd and smiled. "You could not possibly have found a more sympathetic crew than mine. Some of you are from neighboring sectors, in which case getting home will be relatively easy, once you have your bearings. Others of you," and she glanced over at the Nenlars, "have come as far as we have. Your task will be more difficult. But one thing I know in my heart, and that is if we all work together willingly, and share our knowledge freely, we will all benefit.

"Our path leads us into a dangerous area of space. We are determined to traverse it. I wish to formally extend *Voyager*'s companionship, protection, and support to any vessel that wishes to accompany us. For those of you who wish to strike out on your own, I wish you the best of luck. I hope we'll send you on your way better prepared than you might otherwise have been. Now, I would like to invite anyone who cares to to come forward and address the crowd. We'd like to start sharing our knowledge."

There was a lag while the computer translated her speech into the varied languages. Then, all of a sudden, a full quarter of the crowd rose and began marching with purpose toward Janeway.

Inwardly, she groaned. This was going to be harder than she had thought.

Is it working? One Who Is Leader queried with an anxious thought.

Let us find out, replied One Who Masters Technology, a hint of smugness tingeing its thoughts. One Who Is Second and One Who Braves Strangers leaned forward, peering at their viewscreen.

Among themselves, they were simply Us and We. Every other intelligent being in the cosmos was Them and They. Contact was to be avoided when possible, and when it was not avoidable, they called themselves the Ones Who Will Not Be Named. They had ears, but no vocal cords. There was much need early on in their evolution to hear sounds that might warn them of danger: a falling tree, the roar of a predator, the strange noises that passed for communication among other beings not advanced enough to have mastered telepathy. Now, the small holes in their large heads that served for ears were assaulted by a cacophony of sound.

Their eyes were dazzled by an array of beings staggering in their differences. The colors, the noises, the sharp, swift movements—so different from the fluid, graceful motions of the Ones Who Will Not Be Named—assaulted them. One Who Masters Technology and One Who Is Second actually cringed back from the images, fluttering their long fingers in what would, in other species, be a cry of distress.

Truth be told, One Who Is Leader wanted to cringe, too. Only One Who Braves Strangers, who had been trained from birth by others of that skill not to be afraid of alien species so that in the rare cases that contact was necessary someone would be willing to do so, seemed at ease. Leader marveled at its control, and was, as ever, a bit unsettled by it.

If only they had not ventured through that strange gateway! They would be happily examining the stars, inspecting uninhabited worlds, traveling in their peaceful, nurturing silence as they usually did. But they had foolishly gone through, and they were in this strange place, forced to learn what they could through the annoying and frightening jabbering of not just one but *dozens* of strange beings.

With no spoken language of their own, it had taken decades of their best minds working on the problem to evolve a translator that took the chatter of other races and turned it into the mental waves that the Ones Who Will Not Be Named could understand. Masters Technology now worked the controls. Finally, it was able to turn off the intrusive noise. Alien words translated into thoughts bombarded them, dozens at a time, most of them utterly pointless. Still, it was the only way the Ones Who Will Not Be Named could hope to learn anything, and Leader renewed its determination.

CHAPTER
5

SEVEN AND A HALF LONG, LOUD, EXHAUSTING, AND
largely futile hours later, one Captain Kathryn
Janeway slouched back toward her quarters utterly
drained.

"Lights," she called in a voice made hoarse by
screaming to be heard over the din of sixty-two arguing voices. She stumbled to the bathroom and
splashed her face. To categorize today as "stress-
ful" would have been the understatement of the
decade.

The door chimed. She sighed and dried her face.
"Come," she called.

The door hissed open and Chakotay entered.
"When we reach Earth, I'm going to recommend
that you be appointed an ambassador," he said,
amusement warming his voice.

51

"No, thank you," she replied huskily. She went to the replicator. "Vulcan spice tea. Hot. With a touch of honey."

Throwing propriety to the wind, she took a sip of tea, placed it down, and then collapsed on the bed. "That," she said with infinite weariness, "has got to be the single most exhausting day of my life."

"If it's any consolation, Tuvok's contacts reported that the overall tone among the aliens was much calmer after the meeting than beforehand."

"Of course it was," Janeway said. "Everyone was too tired to argue anymore."

Chakotay laughed out loud at that. He sat down next to her on the bed. "You did a wonderful job today. What you had to face was something that I'll wager even Ambassador Spock would have found difficult."

"Thanks," she said, and meant it. She rolled into a seated position and sipped her tea again. Normally she was a coffee woman, but Tuvok had recommended the spiced tea for the sore throat. It was tastier than she imagined and it was definitely soothing.

"Have we heard anything back from any of the ships yet?" she asked, staring pointedly at the padd Chakotay was holding.

"Funny you should ask. Twelve ships have decided that they want nothing to do with any of us. Seventeen are opting to find their own ways home, but thanked us politely for our help. Ten ships have officially agreed to accompany us through No Man's Land, and the rest we haven't heard from yet."

"Who's coming?"

Chakotay again glanced at the padd. "The Nenlars. The Todanians. The Iudka," he said, looking at her.

"That will be interesting," said Janeway. She listened while Chakotay rattled off a lengthy list. "The Salamar. The Lamorians. The Kuluuk. The Iyal. The Yumiri. The Tllihuh. . . ." Sometimes she was able to put names to faces, but most of them were just a blur of odd syllables.

Until he said, "The Hirogen."

She swallowed her mouthful of tea. "I was surprised they would even come to the meeting. The idea of the hunters sitting quietly while surrounded by prey seemed too much to ask for. And now they want to join us?" She raised a skeptical eyebrow. "Perhaps they want a chance to pick us off one by one."

He looked at her searchingly. "That doesn't sound like you."

She sighed. "You're right. It's the exhaustion talking." She put her hand on his arm. "I shouldn't be making important decisions right now. Let's meet in the morning."

He nodded agreement, said good night, and left. She prepared for sleep herself. When she crawled between the sheets, she fell asleep almost immediately. And when she dreamed, it was a busy, restless dream of thousands of people all talking at once, with a terrible danger threatening, and not a one of them listening to his neighbor.

Janeway awoke with the germ of an idea, and the more she thought about it, the better it seemed. The large meeting had, despite the tension, been useful. But what she needed to do was get to know these people, if she was going to be traveling with them. She decided that every night, she would have an informal dinner with a representative or two from a different species. They would, she hoped, feel more relaxed and free to speak about their personal concerns one-on-one without trying to jockey for position in order to be heard.

They had already gotten to know the Nenlar. Janeway decided that the next race she would get to know—and, she resolved, with an open mind—would be the Iudka.

So it was that at 1800, Janeway, Chakotay, and Tuvok stood in the transporter room while Ensign Campbell beamed up the commander of the *Nivvika* and his first officer.

Like the Nenlar that they had terrorized, according to Ara and Torar, the Iudka were humanoid. They were smaller and much slighter than Janeway had mentally pictured them. Their skin glistened like mother-of-pearl, and there was not a hair on their slender forms. Their clothes were loose and brightly colored. Their bearing was proud, but not arrogant, and they understood the humanoid gesture of the smile.

To her surprise, the commander stepped forward with his hand outstretched. "I have been reviewing the information you sent about your culture, Captain Janeway. I understand that this handclasp is a form of greeting. Please instruct me on the finer points, that I may perform it correctly."

Slightly taken aback, Janeway smiled. "We each clasp opposite hands, like so." She accompanied the words with gestures. "We squeeze firmly, but not too tightly, and then we pump the hand up and down a few times."

"Ah. What is the origin of this handclasp?"

Now Janeway had to laugh a little. "It was so that in ancient times, enemies could approach for peace negotiations without fear that the other had a weapon in his hand."

The commander looked rueful. "As is so often the case, it was born from suspicion. Nonetheless, it is a pleasant form of greeting. I am Commander Kelmar. This is my First Officer, Second Commander Lel. We are delighted to be aboard your magnificent vessel."

Janeway considered herself a pretty good judge of character, and there was nothing about these two that bespoke a nature that would enjoy the atrocities that the Nenlar attributed to them.

It was going to be an interesting dinner.

Neelix had asked for, and been sent, several recipes native to the Iudka. Janeway had insisted that he replicate the food rather than cooking it himself. To cheer him up, she had told him that if he wished, he could perform the task of headwaiter, which seemed to delight him no end. Neelix reveled in getting to know people, and to have him serve the food would be an excellent way to include him in these dinners without making him an official guest. Oftentimes, flies on the wall heard more.

He stood eagerly awaiting them in Janeway's quarters. "Good evening, Commander, First Officer. Please, do have a seat."

"This is Mr. Neelix, our sometime ambassador

and resident chef," said Janeway. "If the food is to your liking, he gets the credit."

"And the blame if it's not," said Chakotay teasingly.

"Ah, ah," and Neelix waggled a remonstrative finger. "Let's try it first, shall we?"

They took their seats. Neelix began serving some kind of purple soup with odd-shaped lumps. It did, however, smell heavenly.

"*Carmor* soup!" exclaimed Kelmar with delight. "I haven't had this in a long time. *Carmor* testicles are so difficult to come by."

Janeway froze with the spoon halfway to her mouth. She hesitated, and then grimly began to eat. She had to admit it wasn't half bad.

"We have technology that enables us to replicate any dish for which we know the recipe," said Chakotay. He seemed to have no problems with *carmor* testicles in his soup. But now that she looked closer, the "testicles" looked suspiciously like pasta. "I'm sure it's not the same as homemade, but we try."

Kelmar did not reply; his mouth was full.

The fine start to the dinner only continued. Neelix had two more courses, some synthale patterned after Iudka wine, and a dessert that was so sweet Janeway could manage only a few mouthfuls. The discussion stayed mainly on safe topics. Janeway learned about her guests' children and families, how the Iukda elected their officials, their fondness for a peculiar game called *ijik,* which involved three balls, seven sticks, and apparently lots of yelling, and the *Nivvika*'s journey up to this point. After dinner, the captain herself brought a pot of Neelix's best coffee substitute to the table and graciously poured for her guests.

"This is one of our delicacies," she informed them. "It's a mild stimulant. I hope you enjoy it."

They sipped, and pronounced it good, though Lel put about six spoonfuls of sugar into his. Heartened, Janeway decided that it was time to bring up more serious topics.

"As you no doubt are aware," she began pleasantly, "we have two representatives here from a race known to your people. They are Ara and Torar, and they are from Nenlar."

She watched them closely. Kelmar stiffened. "Yes," he said heavily. "We know. And let me guess. They have told you tales of atrocities perpetrated on their people by mine. They told you stories of plunder and senseless, vindictive destruction. They told you that we are monsters, and that they have spent the intervening centuries simply trying to rebuild their world and live a peaceful life."

"Yes," said Chakotay, obviously surprised. "They have."

Here it comes, thought Janeway. *The explanations, the excuses, all the "reasons" for why they did what they did, or maybe just flat-out denial.*

"They told you the truth about us," Kelmar said bluntly. Janeway raised an eyebrow. She hadn't been expecting that.

"Our ancestors were indeed monstrous in their treatment of other worlds. The Nenlar have company for their grievances against the Iudka. We once saw other worlds as our own, and took what we wanted from them. Alien lives were reckoned no more precious than those of the beasts we bred and slaughtered for our food. The galaxy was nothing but a countless array of presents for the Iudka, and anyone who tried to stand in our way suffered terribly. If memory serves me correctly—there are so many races who have suffered at our hands, you must forgive me if I cannot recall all the details—they were the race that first gave us the *annarium*." He turned to Lel for confirmation.

"I think so, yes," said Lel.

Kelmar turned back to Janeway. "We took everything that we could use, and then we bombed the planet. It was a routine procedure in those days. I do not deny our past, Captain. And I do not wax eloquent about any specious 'lost glory.' Our ancestors were unevolved brutes. We realize that the path to advancement lies in peaceful coexistence, not destruction and war. And we have turned our efforts toward healing the damage that was done so long ago. But," and his voice was hard, "you need to understand two things, Captain Janeway. I cannot be held responsible for what someone several centuries ago did. I can regret those actions, but I will not apologize. *I* have never authorized wanton destruction, and therefore *I* won't bow my head and have stones flung at me for what some stranger did in the past."

"Fair enough," said Janeway.

"And also, the Nenlar may have been terribly wronged at one point, but they too have blood on their hands. Many of them are terrorists. They have no uniform government declaring war, but many individuals have devoted their lives to exacting some kind of retribution for what their ancestors suffered. These terrorists do not fight openly, but in stealth, in darkness, with a coward's ways and a coward's weapons. And frankly, in all honesty it is a tiny percentage of the population. I do not hate the Nenlar, but neither can I call them utterly innocent. I imagine the Nenlars you spoke with did not mention this."

"No," said Tuvok. "They did not."

"I am not at all surprised." Kelmar sank back and sipped at his coffee. "Captain, I have no desire to stir up ancient enmity. I will happily cooperate with any of the ships that choose to join this caravan, including the Nenlar. But I'm not here to negotiate a peace agreement. If they will leave us alone, and respect our ways, I can guarantee my crew will behave in the same manner."

"Given the circumstances," said Janeway, "that's all anyone could ask for."

Kelmar nodded, once. He seemed satisfied. "Now, Mr. Neelix," he said to the Talaxian, who had been quietly standing by observing, "you said something about a beverage called Saurian brandy?"

When a sleepy-looking Ara appeared on the viewscreen in Janeway's private quarters, the captain of *Voyager* minced no words.

"I don't take kindly to being lied to."

Ara seemed totally shocked. "Captain, I do not understand. We have not lied to you about anything." Torar moved into the picture.

"I just had dinner with Kelmar and Lel, commander and first officer of the Iudka vessel," Janeway continued, watching their reactions closely. As she expected, they seemed horrified that she would consort with such creatures. She plowed on.

"Kelmar freely admits to what his people did to yours in the past. And it sounds like the present Iudka governments are sorry for what happened and don't behave like that any longer. However, he told us something interesting about certain branches of the Nenlar. He used the word 'terrorist.' Was he lying?"

Torar sighed heavily. "No," he said. "But they are such a small, wayward group—Captain, you know how fearful we are. To overcome the fear and turn it against an old enemy would take something that few of my people have. I would say it is only one in several hundred thousand, perhaps one in a million. And we are not a populous people."

Janeway's heart softened as she looked at them. They were trembling with fear. Or was it fear of discovery? Perhaps these two were of the admittedly rare few that could overcome their fear. Her mind raced with dark scenarios.

Finally, she sighed. She was not about to condemn either race out of hand. How they behaved on this journey would determine how she regarded them.

"Kelmar says that as long as you leave him and his people alone, and show them respect, he will guarantee the same behavior."

The two Nenlars exchanged glances, but finally Ara nodded. "If he truly holds to that, then we will happily agree to stay as far away from him and his ship as we may."

"Very well, then. Good night." The screen went dark. Janeway rubbed her tired eyes.

Day Two was proving to be as exhausting as Day One. And they hadn't even started on No Man's Land yet. Tomorrow would be the first official leg of the journey, provided everyone's vessel was ready.

She was not looking forward to it. She reached out a hand for a padd and thumbed it. She had requested a meeting with the Hirogen next. The following day, it would be with a race called the Todanians. A faint memory stirred. She closed her eyes and concentrated and a hard, angry voice floated back to her: *"This is Leader Sinimar Arkathi, of the Todanian vessel the* Relka. *We demand to know why you have brought us here."*

No. She definitely was not looking forward to tomorrow.

Torar stared at the screen long after it had ceased to show the angry face of Captain Janeway. Ara finally placed a hand on his shoulder.

"Don't worry," she soothed her mate. "If she suspected, she would act."

"Would she?" asked Torar, leaning back in his chair. "Or would she wait, and watch, and let us think she believes us to be the cowards we portrayed ourselves as?"

"It doesn't matter. We talked about this," said Ara, sliding into the chair next to him. "We agreed we would not attempt anything. It would be too obvious. There are too many witnesses."

Torar growled, deep in his throat. "It took me

years to put my anger before my fear. Even now, it takes a deliberate effort. We were not born for hate and fighting. But we have to follow those paths, Ara."

"Of course we do," she agreed, "but not here, not now. Let us return home, in one piece. Perhaps by feigning friendship or at the least tolerance we may learn something to aid us in our battle against the Iudka."

He touched her face. "Do you speak wisdom, or cowardice, Ara? I'm not sure anymore. I'm not sure of anything, except that to know that the Iudka are so close and not to do anything is eating me up inside."

"I speak wisdom, beloved. There is a time and place for everything. We can resume our attacks when we are safely home. For now, be at peace with this."

"I will try to be at peace," Torar agreed, "for now. But I do not know how long that peace will last."

Marisha's lungs heaved as she attempted to exert the required strength to adjust the engines. The air, as always, was too thin. She wondered how many times this same scenario had repeated itself. It was a wonder she was not dead. She had seen so many of her compatriots die here, in the hot, foul-smelling innards of the ship their masters owned. They lay where they had fallen, their decaying bodies adding their own terrible stench, until a "sweeper" came every few days to remove the corpses and expel them into space, much as they might refuse that no longer concerned them.

Marisha had come to labor on this vessel five years ago, when she was still very young. She had grown to adulthood here, and she knew that it was unlikely that she would ever see anything other than these walls, know anything other than brutal, harsh conditions.

Others were meek as *timkas*. They were born, they worked, and they died. That was their lot. But Marisha's mother had escaped once, had seen a world other than this, and had whispered stories of that other world into her daughter's small, shell-shaped ear. And so Marisha, unlike nearly every other V'enah she had ever met, hungered for something more.

It was this hunger, this fire, that kept her sane. That kept her thinking, alert, outraged at the life she was being forced to live. At first, she had said nothing to her fellow slaves. But they had sensed it. Marisha had always been a leader, even as a child. The other V'enah flocked to her as if trying to warm their cold souls at her inner flame. After a few years, she began to speak, softly, about that other world of which her mother had spoken. They listened. And finally, just recently, Marisha had ventured into speaking of that most elusive of dreams . . . freedom.

Her hand touched sizzling metal. She uttered a wordless cry and jerked it back, hissing in pain as she examined the burned flesh. She took a deep breath and willed herself not to think of the pain. There would be no point. There was no way to heal it. The Todanians would not waste precious supplies on expendable V'enah.

Except, she had heard something from the guards about a portal. Of course, she had seen nothing. None of those laboring in the ship's innards had. But they were not in Todanian space now, and perhaps the V'enah would be more precious now that the Todanians could not resupply living labor in the same fashion as they would food or water.

At precisely that moment, one of the ugly, hulking guards approached. His lip curled in a sneer, but he thrust something at her. Confused, she stared at it. She did not dare speak.

"Salve," the guard grunted. "Put it on and wrap it in the bandage."

When she did not take it immediately, he growled. He seized her wrist, smeared something vile-smelling on it, and wrapped the bandage around the injury. He jerked the ends tight and tied them, eliciting another cry from Marisha.

"Our orders are to take care of you vermin, now that we're lost," he said with contempt. Tears welled in Marisha's eyes; not emotional tears, for she was beyond that, but a simple physical reaction to the pain in her hand. "Enjoy it while it lasts."

Marisha did not move as the guard threaded his way through the stunned crowd of V'enah. When he was out of sight, she rewrapped the bandage so it did not cut viciously into her flesh. Regardless of the lack of care with which the guard had given her the treatment, it was working. Already her hand felt better. She could even see the inflammation start to recede. It was an odd sensation.

For the briefest of moments, she felt a wave of gratitude. The tears slipped down her pale purple cheeks. They cared. They wanted to treat her well. They—

They were monsters. The only reason they treated her was because they wanted her alive to work harder for them. This was no selfless act of compassion. If anything, it was worse than the usual, thoughtless treatment the Todanians showed their property.

Marisha returned to her work with a renewed sense of purpose.

The opportunity she had dreamed of for so long was approaching.

CHAPTER

6

JANEWAY DEPLORED PREJUDICE. SHE REJECTED IT WITH every cell in her body. And yet, even as Leader Sinimar Arkathi of the Todanian vessel the *Relka* materialized, she made a prejudgment about him. She didn't like him.

Of course, there was his rude "greeting" before she'd met him. And some of the other species she had met had muttered something about the Todanians. But it was seeing him stand with an air of utter arrogance on her transporter platform, staring about as if he owned the ship, that got her hackles up. He was bipedal, but not exactly humanoid. He reminded her of a frog, with large, bulging eyes and a thick mouth. But no frog had the rippling muscles and thick fur that the Todanians had, and no simple beast showed such calculated hostility in its bearing.

"Captain Janeway. I am Leader Arkathi. You will show me the rest of your ship."

She bit back a retort and smiled pleasantly instead. "I'm flattered that you take such an interest in my ship," she said, forcing her voice to be mild and pleasant. "But our dinner is waiting. Follow me, please."

It didn't get better after that. Nothing was to the Todanians' taste. The wine was bitter. The grubs weren't alive. The soup was thin. The grains were too chewy, the meat too rare, the dessert too sweet. Arkathi actually spat out the single mouthful of coffee he took onto the saucer. Janeway supposed she ought to be grateful he didn't simply spew it onto her, Tuvok, and Chakotay even as she lamented the waste of good coffee. All her attempts at polite conversation were brushed aside with blunt replies or stony silence.

She was no longer a narrow-minded, prejudiced person. She had interacted enough with Arkathi to make a reasoned judgment based on gathered data.

And she didn't like him.

She decided to be as blunt as he. "From the information you sent me," she began, thinking even as she spoke that it was in truth very little information, "I understand that you have two species working on your vessel. I'm curious as to why you chose to bring four Todanians and no V'enah. We ourselves have a multispecies crew and I enjoy displaying the variety of talents we have at our disposal when we're interacting with new races."

The request had been for two, the commander of each ship and one other. Arkathi, of course, had ignored the request and brought three hulking companions with him, all of whom seemed to be eating vast quantities of the food even while complaining about the quality.

Arkathi stiffened in his seat. The bulging eyes seemed to grow even larger with indignation. "You insult me, Janeway," he said, insulting her in return by not using her title.

She kept calm. "I fail to see how inquiring about more than fifty percent of your crew is an insult, Arkathi."

"The V'enah are not crew! They are property!"

Janeway hoped that the translator had somehow misunderstood the word. "Property? Are you telling me that the Todanians *own* the V'enah?"

"Precisely. And we have for centuries. They have no business representing my vessel."

"But they do all the hard labor, don't they?" She knew she was treading on thin ice, but she didn't care.

"Of course. That's what they're bred for. Now, on to what we will require of you." To Janeway's shock he pulled out a small device that was clearly their version of a padd. "We require assistance in repairing the damage we incurred on traversing the portal. We were well supplied for our brief mission, but will of course now require foodstuffs if we are to offer you our company and protection. We—"

"Stop it right there." Chakotay's voice was mild, though his words were sharp. His dark face was darker than usual with anger, though his expression didn't change. "We are in charge of this mission. We invited you to accompany us, not to protect us, or escort us. We are not in your debt in any way."

"You can choose to travel with us," Janeway said, "to have the protection and resources of a caravan available, or not. I can tell you it matters very little to me." Janeway knew as she spoke that her words were hardly diplomatic, but she didn't care. There were many others to worry about, not least her own crew. "But if you choose to come with us, you will regard *Voyager* as the flagship. You will follow our route, at our pace, and you will take instructions from me in case of any trouble. Is that clear?"

For a moment, she thought he was going to explode. It was a measure of her distaste for Arkathi that the only problem she saw with that scenario would be getting what was left out of the carpeting. He swelled up, and inflated two large, bright red sacs on each side of his throat.

Janeway waited.

Finally, Arkathi spoke. "You have made your arrogant position extremely clear, Captain." He threw down the napkin and rose. His three companions rose with him. One of them—she remembered his name was Sook—at least had the grace to look embarrassed. The foursome stalked out, with Sook casting a quick, backward glance before lifting his head as high as his leader's.

"The turbolift is on your left," Janeway called after them, then rubbed her aching head.

"Captain," began Tuvok, "if I may—"

"You may not. I know if that had been a scenario test at the Academy, I'd have failed miserably. But frankly, if the Todanians are going to be such unpleasant traveling companions, I'd just as soon they struck off on their own."

But she was to have no such luck. The following day, they received a message, as curt and to the point as Janeway would have expected: *We will travel with you.*

"Damn," she said to herself. At once she amended the thought. *Think of the V'enah on that ship,* she thought. *They've got no choice but to be here. Perhaps we can serve to enlighten their "masters." At the very least, we can do what we can to make the journey easier on them by not taxing the Todanians too much.*

The thought wasn't much comfort.

They are moving forward.

Leader nodded, acknowledging Second. It had dreaded this, even as it knew such a thing would eventually occur. Now Leader had to decide. Did the Ones Who Will Not Be Named follow the caravan, undetected and cautious? Or did they strike out on their own, avoiding any possible chance of discovery or pollution from this constant monitoring of the hordes of alien species?

Its instinct told Leader to flee. Better wandering the stars alone, lost forever, than trailing these ships and filling their minds with alien madness.

But its powerful brain said otherwise. One of the ships had been lost for years here, and was making obvious progress toward its home sector. Perhaps they knew what they were doing. At the very least, with so many other ships going ahead of them, the

Ones Who Will Not Be Named would stand a better chance of avoiding the dangers that they knew lurked ahead.

Finally, Leader made its decision.

We will follow.

Captain's log, stardate 53701.4. I had thought that actually traversing No Man's Land would be the true challenge, but I am now starting to believe that we will encounter more difficulties simply getting along with the rest of this odd caravan. Last night, it was the Todanians. Tonight we have the Hirogen. I hope I am up to the task.

Neelix couldn't wait. He was fairly quivering with excitement when Seven brought in the four Borg children to join him and Naomi in the mess hall. Paris was already there, having taken a shine to the strange little animal. It was currently frolicking about, sniffing everything and begging for attention.

"I'm thinking about calling him . . . Fluffy," Neelix said with paternal pride.

"Fluffy?" Tom looked aghast. "Don't saddle him with that kind of a name."

"What kind of a name? He's very fluffy. It fits."

"Yeah, if that's the best you can think of. Why not something that really honors the little guy?" Paris picked him up and Fluffy/Unnamed stuck out a black tongue to lick his face. "You want a *good* name, don't you? Hmm?"

The little animal barked, its tail wagging furiously. Paris's face lit up.

"That's it! I've got the name for him! Barkley!"

"After Reginald Barclay?" Neelix frowned, pondering the choice. "Well, he did show up soon after our contact with Barclay, and he is an honorary member of the crew. . . ."

"No, you don't get it. *Bark*-ley. As in, a dog bark." Paris was terribly pleased with himself. "Terrific name, huh? It honors our discoverer and it's a great pun!"

Neelix didn't think it was so great a pun. "Barkley" indeed. "Fluffy" was much better, much more suitable. He took the dog from Paris's arms and handed it to Naomi, whose little face broke into a big grin.

"Which name do you like best, sweetie?" he asked.

"Aw, come on, don't put the pressure on the kid," said Paris. At that moment, the door hissed open and Seven entered with the four Borg children. They stepped in a few paces, spotted Naomi holding Fluffy/Barkley, and halted.

"Canine," Mezoti said. "Carnivore. Irrelevant." She looked up at Seven. "You brought us here to encounter one of these?"

"Neelix suggested that you might like to play with this species," said Seven, in a voice that suggested that she cared as little for the idea as Mezoti did.

"I'd rather return to my studies," said Icheb.

"Fun is an integral part of a healthy and well-rounded childhood," said Seven, grimly. "We shall have fun now."

At a nod from Neelix, Naomi set Fluffy/Barkley on the floor. At once it scampered toward the newcomers, then skidded to a halt. It began to bark furiously.

"Perceptive creature," muttered Paris under his breath.

Rebi looked at the creature. "Can we go now?"

"Yes, can we go?" echoed Azan.

"Negative. We will interact with Species 775."

"His name is Barkley," said Paris.

"No, it's Fluffy!" retorted Neelix. "He's a pet—a domesticated creature. He needs play, and so do you five. Oh, come on, you've got to admit he's cute."

"Cute is irrelevant," stated Mezoti.

"Cute," said Paris, quite firmly, "is *never* irrelevant."

"Seven," said Icheb, "I anticipate difficulty in interacting in a logical fashion with Species 775." Barkley/Fluffy continued to bark. Seven sighed, reached down, and picked him up. The animal quieted at once. She held it out at arm's length, scrutinizing it.

"Soft, long hair. Appealing large eyes. Enjoyment of touch. The animal is cute."

There was silence. Neelix was reminded of ambassadors negotiating a peace treaty. Finally, Mezoti looked up at Seven.

"Seven, how do we . . . play?"

"Like this," said Naomi helpfully. She sat down on the floor and at once Fluffy/Barkley bounced happily over toward her. She stroked his head. He immediately rolled over onto his back.

"See? He wants you to pet his tummy," said Naomi, proceeding to suit action to word. One of Barkley/Fluffy's hind legs began to kick frantically.

"Species—Fluffy is demonstrating that he is submissive to you," said Seven. "He regards you as a dominant pack leader."

"And *Barkley* also wants his tummy scratched," said Tom, stooping down to join Naomi.

For a long moment, the Borg children stood as if bolted to the deck. Then, finally, Mezoti sat down awkwardly next to Naomi.

"How does one handle the creature?" she asked.

Naomi smiled. "Gently, but with a lot of affection. Like this." She stroked Fluffy/Barkley's head. Tentatively, Mezoti followed suit, moving her small hand in a cautious rhythm over the creature's skull.

Rebi was next, then Azan, and finally, after a look at Seven, Icheb. Barkley/Fluffy was obviously in doggie heaven, with all these attentive children. Neelix hoped he wouldn't get so excited he wet the floor. At one point, Fluffy/Barkley bounded into Mezoti's lap, stood on his hind legs, planted his forelegs on her shoulder, and furiously licked her face. The girl started for a moment, then laughed.

Neelix's heart felt very full. It was the first time he had seen one of these traumatized children laugh, like a child ought.

"We can call him Barkley if it's that important to you, Tom," he said, filled with warm generosity at this moment.

Paris, too, was gazing at the children with a rapt expression on his face. "No, Neelix. You're the one taking care of him. We'll call him Fluffy."

"No, no, I insist. Barkley it is."

Tom looked up at him. "Fluffy," he said, with an edge to his voice.

Neelix sighed.

* * *

Sinimar Arkathi sat alone in his quarters. The bottle had been full an hour ago; now it was almost empty. He picked it up, swirled the light orange contents about, and wished he had thought to pack another seven crates of the stuff.

Things had gone badly from the very beginning of this mission. He had gotten the position of Leader only because of a rift between the Magla Karn and his advisory council. Arkathi knew he had been chosen not for his skill or experience or other positive qualities, but because his appointment would irritate the advisory council. He was, therefore, the commander of a ship on the whim of one powerful man, and he knew it.

Grimly, Arkathi poured the last of the liquid into the heavy goblet. He sniffed the spicy aroma, and took a deep drink. Fire coursed through his system, but it did not relax him as it used to.

His crew knew it, too. Even the cursed V'enah had somehow got wind of the fact that the commander of the *Relka* was a choice of spite.

"Kella!" he called. The door hissed open. A small female V'enah entered. At once, she dropped to her hands and knees, making herself as small as possible in his august presence.

"Master," she said in a little voice, not looking up. "How can I serve you?"

"More *olifir*. And then a massage and a bath."

"As my master wills," said Kella, again in that soft, whispery voice. She rose to her feet and disappeared, only to return a moment later with a fresh bottle. Arkathi drained what was left in the goblet and wordlessly thrust it out for a refill. With the expertise of long practice, Kella, kneeling on the floor, opened the bottle and poured. She did not, of course, take any herself. Woe be unto the Todanian who dared let a V'enah taste the richness of *olifir.*

On a whim, he decided to test his theory. "What have you heard about me?" he demanded.

Kella kept her eyes averted, but could not hide the telltale rush of blood to her cheeks that colored them a deep purple hue. "I am not certain what my master means."

"What are they saying about me? The V'enah. What are they saying about their captain?"

"The V'enah are your loyal servants, Master. We would never—"

Arkathi swore an oath so blistering it startled even Kella, who had heard him swear often. "That's a lie and we both know it. They talk. I want to know what they say." Yielding to impulse, he leaned forward and squeezed her chin in his massive hand. She uttered one soft cry, and then was silent, her gaze stubbornly lowered.

"What do they say, Kella? The truth, now, or I shall have you put back in engineering with the others."

It was an empty threat. Kella was the perfect personal attendant: quiet, obedient, attractive enough for her species, and very good at untying the knots of stress that accumulated in his body. He once thought about bedding her. She couldn't refuse, but he simply couldn't bring himself to think of a V'enah's body lying next to his.

But Kella didn't know that. And he never intended her to know just how valuable she was to him. Let her think he would toss her into the killing room, as it was commonly known. It would ensure that obedience he so prized.

"I—they—truly, Master, I do not have much contact with the others," she stammered.

That much at least was fact. Still . . .

"What little I have heard . . . surely, Master, these are rumors only, and unworthy of passing on to your most noble ears. . . ."

He squeezed tighter. There would be bruises on that pretty face. But he had to know.

"They say that you were gifted this assignment. That it was the result of some kind of conflict. But I know that you earned it, Master!"

He let her go. If even the V'enah knew this, then everyone on board knew it. Kella got to her feet and disappeared. He heard water hissing as she drew his bath. She would scent it with herbs to make it fragrant, lave his body with oils to make both his skin and fur soft. But his mind was not on the upcoming bath or massage. It was on how to turn himself into a true leader in the eyes of his people.

And that way was to knock the leader of this expedition, one Captain Kathryn Janeway, out of the top seat.

Kella came out of the room, again dropping to all fours. He could already see the darkness on her face from the pressure of his fingers. Regrettable, but necessary. He'd have their doctor remove the bruises in the morning. It would be a gift from a beneficent master to a loyal slave, and she would be grateful.

He finished the glass of *olifir*, staggered to his feet, and lurched toward the bathing room.

As she bathed the loathed, bumpy body of the being who owned her, her face aching from his abuse, Kella wished with all her heart that she had the courage to seize the bottle of *olifir* and crack it against Arkathi's skull.

But she did not. And so she bathed him, and massaged him, and went to her sleeping mat at the foot of his bed with pain, fear, and hatred all at war in her two-chambered heart.

CHAPTER

7

JANEWAY HAD FORGOTTEN JUST HOW BIG THE HIROGEN were.

These two were massive specimens of their species. Two and a half meters tall, both of them, if they were a centimeter. They came in full armor, their small, dark eyes almost the only part of their bodies visible beneath the blue-black, spiked shell. Her eyes flickered up to their helmets, searching for the paint that she knew would signify that they were on the hunt.

There was no paint. And for that, she was grateful.

She had spoken only briefly with them, and then only about the specifics of the mission. She hoped that tonight she would learn more about their behavior, so peculiar for this race of self-proclaimed hunters. They had made no aggressive moves whatsoever, and, as always when people or species acted out of character, that made her suspicious.

"Welcome aboard *Voyager*," she said, inclining her head in the gesture that she knew showed respect.

There was a hesitation; then the bigger one nodded. The second, the Beta, followed suit. They remained silent.

Janeway raised an eyebrow, then said, "Our meal is waiting. If you will accompany me."

It was more difficult than she had expected, turning her back on the two hulking beings, trusting them to follow as honored guests. Tuvok had wanted to post a security guard, but Janeway had refused. Thus far, the Hirogen had offered no hostility, she'd told the Vulcan. She was not going to give them any reason to think they'd been mistaken.

"As far as I'm concerned, every ship out there is an ally," she'd stated firmly. An easy statement to make in the comfort and security of her ready room. Not so easy to hold to now, with no phaser at her hip and two enormous Hirogen striding behind her.

The walk to her quarters from the transporter room, necessitating a brief trip in the turbolift, which felt crowded though there were only three of them, seemed to take forever. Her shoulder blades tingled, as if expecting to feel a knife. But of course, no strike came.

Tuvok, Neelix, and Chakotay were already in her quarters. They all nodded, as she'd told them to do. She made the introductions.

"Please sit down. Make yourselves comfortable."

They did so. Thus far, they had said nothing. Janeway hoped that once the wine started flowing more freely, the conversation would as well. She amended the thought. She didn't dare hope for free-flowing conversation; *anything* other than "Pass the salt" would do.

"You may wish to remove your helmets," said Chakotay as Neelix began to pour the synthetic wine.

Again, they looked at each other, and wordlessly complied with Chakotay's suggestion. The faces that the gesture revealed were unattractive to Janeway's personal aesthetics. The ridges along their faces that differentiated from individual to individual looked like scabs to her, and their eyes were unsettling.

Janeway picked up her glass. "It is the custom among our people to salute our guests. We call this form of salutation a toast. Please, lift your glasses." They did so, in that same stony silence. "To cooperation between species. May this be the beginning of a new, better relationship between our peoples."

She and her crew began to drink, but the Hirogen put their glasses down. "Something the matter, gentlemen?"

"Let me speak plainly," said the Alpha. His voice was harsh and gravelly, almost mechanical-sounding. "Simply because we have accepted your invitation to dine aboard your vessel does not mean we are interested in bettering relationships. We are the hunters. You are, and always will be, prey to us."

She'd expected this much, and was oddly relieved by his words. Now, at least, they were talking, and she'd always preferred open hostility and confrontation to the lie and the knife in the back.

"Your words don't really surprise me," she said, "though I must confess I'm disappointed. Why did you accept? And why are you not offering any threat to any other vessel here? This must be terribly exciting to you. You have flying right next to your ship prey from far distant parts of the galaxy. They would be wonderful relics. Why are you not hunting us?"

Unobtrusively, Neelix began serving soup. Janeway noticed there were two different sets of bowls and was suddenly terribly grateful to the Talaxian. She knew that the Hirogen dissolved their prey and fed upon them, after recovering their gruesome "relics." In the interest of science, they had saved some of the recipes that the Hirogen had programmed into the replicator when *Voyager* had been captured and boarded and her crew forced to play holodeck games of violence. Neelix had obviously prepared appropriate meals for their guests, but what was in front of her, judging by the aroma, was nothing more than good old-fashioned split-pea soup.

"Only a fool tries to hunt when he could be the hunted," said Alpha. He spooned up some of the soup. "Delicious," he said, sounding a bit surprised.

"Some of your kind once captured our vessel," began Janeway, but Alpha interrupted.

"I am aware of that. As I said, we know of you, Captain. And of your holodeck technology." He stared at her with unreadable brown eyes. "I condemn such technology. The Alpha may have thought he was helping to preserve our way of life, but a holodeck simulation is not the same as an actual kill. It can never be the same."

"Don't knock it till you've tried it," said Chakotay, spooning up his split-pea soup.

"I have no desire to try it," said the Alpha. He continued eating.

They finished the soup course in silence. Neelix brought out a replicated haunch of some unidentifiable creature. Janeway wondered what it was supposed to be. It smelled like lamb to her. As hostess, she stood and began to carve.

"If you know of the incident," said Tuvok, "then you must be aware that we are a formidable foe. That conflict ended in a cease-fire."

"Only because the Alpha and Beta of the vessel were weak and feebleminded," said the Beta, speaking up for the first time. "You will not find that to be the case with us."

"Rare or well done?" Janeway asked with false pleasantness. They did not reply, so she served up the pieces as she sliced them.

"But you have said that only a fool hunts when he could be the hunted," said Chakotay.

"Of course," said Alpha. "There is a time and place for hunting, and now is not it. We are outnumbered at least sixty to one, perhaps more, Commander. Your ship alone could destroy our tiny vessel. We do not know this area of space. You are offering to get us through it alive. Only a madman would try to fight in such circumstances."

"As long as we're in No Man's Land, then, do we have your word that you will cooperate?" Janeway's voice was soft, but her eyes were intent upon Alpha as she asked the question.

"Yes," stated Alpha firmly. "No one in this caravan need fear an attack by the Hirogen. We will even go so far as to offer what expertise and technology we can for the betterment of the group."

"It may be discourteous of me to doubt the offer,"

said Tuvok. "But I cannot help but think that this situation is rife with temptation for your species."

"I believe them," said Chakotay, unexpectedly. "You're hunters. You respect the prey. And you respect your own safety. Without prey, you cannot be a predator. In the twentieth century on my home planet, hunters were some of the most active individuals in preserving the species they hunted. During bad winters, they were out placing down food for the creature they planned to hunt months later. It's a circle."

"You do understand," said Alpha, a hint of respect on his ugly visage.

"We will take your word," said Janeway. "But remember, if you break it, you will lose any protection this caravan and my ship can offer."

"I hear you, Captain Janeway," said Alpha. He cut into the meat on his plate. She had given him a rare slice, and blood dripped from the fork. Alpha took a bite and nodded his approval.

"This flesh," he said, "is savory."

"Bridge to Janeway. We're about to enter."

Janeway's heart sped up a little more. She was in her ready room, poring through exhaustive reports from all the various species who were part of this odd group. She'd asked Chakotay to notify her when they were about to enter the first dangerous stretch of No Man's Land.

She entered, and gazed at the screen.

"There it is," said Chakotay softly.

Janeway didn't say anything for a moment. They were poised on the brink, now, as they had been so many times before. They stood ready to enter territory utterly unfamiliar to them, beset with dangers known and unknown. She never made the decision to take her ship into possible danger lightly. But this time, even more was riding on her decisions. She was, in effect, the commander of a small, vulnerable, frightened fleet. She had asked these people, liked and disliked, to trust in her, and they had done so.

"Seven of Nine to Captain Janeway."

Inwardly, Janeway groaned as she took her seat. "Go ahead, Seven."

"I regret to say I have bad news," said Seven.

Janeway closed her eyes, gathering strength. "And I haven't even finished my morning coffee yet."

"Shall I wait until you have done so?"

Janeway smiled to herself. Sometimes Seven was so literal. "No, go ahead."

"There is a great deal of the spatial distortion activity occurring within—within No Man's Land. It is causing repercussions on the various other spatial phenomena in the area."

"Such as?" Janeway threw Chakotay a glance. She was beginning to wish she *had* waited to have that cup of coffee before hearing this.

"The trajectory of the comets we charted has been altered. The nebula has shifted to bearing eight zero mark four point two. The—"

"Point taken. We'll proceed at half impulse until you've had a chance to map it out more completely. In the meantime, we'll just have to take it as it comes."

There was no way Janeway was going to wait any longer. The small fleet she captained was champing at the bit to get going. Even half impulse would require that they pay close attention. It would keep them from getting restless and deciding to pick fights among themselves.

"Mr. Kim, open a channel."

"Channel opened, Captain."

"This is Captain Kathryn Janeway to all vessels. We are about to proceed into the dangerous area of space we discussed earlier. Because of the activity of the portals that brought so many of you here, we will have to remap the area as we go. Our vessel will proceed at half impulse power. We will automatically relay all information we receive to all of you the moment we know it. No one will be kept in the dark. However, no one is to venture out of the prescribed course we will be following. You are all here voluntarily, and I regard you as equals on this journey. However, you have all also agreed that *Voyager* will take the lead. I expect all of you to honor that agreement. Is everyone ready?"

She waited while all of them—twenty-nine ships thus far—responded. Finally, she nodded to herself.

"Then let us begin. Janeway out. Mr. Paris, half impulse. Take us into No Man's Land."

"Yes, ma'am," replied Tom lightly, and touched the controls. Janeway glanced down at her personal viewscreen. She saw dozens of blips of light of various sizes, all moving together.

She hoped they would all make it the same way.

Even though she knew what to expect, even though she was fully aware that there was nothing uncanny or magical about these strange gateways, she felt unsettled every time one of them opened or closed. There had to be a scientific reason for them.

Her crew and all the others who had chosen to accompany *Voyager* on this dangerous trek weren't superstitious primitives. They simply didn't *know* the reason for why these things kept opening and closing. She desperately wished they did, or at least could predict—

"Hard to port!" Janeway cried, even as Tuvok began, "Captain . . ."

Her eyes had caught the telltale ripple that preceded the opening of another door, and this one was far too close for comfort. Paris obeyed, and the ship lurched violently, barely avoiding flying right into the thing.

"That one was close," said Tom. His words were unnecessary. Janeway's own heart was beating rapidly and she trembled from released adrenaline.

"Harry, channel."

"Open."

"Janeway to the fleet. Be forewarned, these gateways keep opening without warning. We narrowly missed flying straight into one. Please have someone on your vessel monitoring sensors at all times. There is also a visual signal, a ripple—"

"Just like that one," cried Kim.

Sure enough, another one was opening right behind them. "Onscreen," Janeway snapped.

A small vessel was traveling close to the gateway. It was as if Janeway were watching the entire thing unfold in slow motion. Even as she shouted, "Bearing eight-four-six-three mark nine," the little ship, unable to halt in time, floated through.

The gateway closed as if it had never been.

"All stop! Full fleet, all stop!" she cried. Seconds

ticked by. Who had it been? She tried to remember, but there were so many of them. Yes, it was the Ammunii. Half the size of humans, quadripedal, using delicate mouths and tentacles to manipulate their vessel. Humor and an immense acceptance and love of all other living beings were qualities that were prized among their people, and they had even given Janeway a gift of a beautiful sphere that was mined on their planet. She'd put the lovely thing in a place of honor in her quarters. She had hoped to invite the young Ammunii over to play; she'd heard that Fluffy, or was it Barkley, was very popular with the children. . . .

"Maybe they made it somewhere safe," said Paris, his voice awkwardly breaking the strained silence.

"Maybe," said Kim, in as stilted and tight a voice.

Suddenly the gateway opened again.

The dead ship floated out.

It was charred, and broken, and somehow . . . aged. If she hadn't known better, Janeway would have put the Ammunii vessel at two, maybe three centuries old. But it had only gone through half a minute ago.

No one spoke. Then Kim's station came alive with the voices of frightened people all trying to speak at once.

Janeway ignored the babble. "Kim, any life signs on the Ammunii ship?"

A pause. "No, Captain."

Janeway bit her lip. She then signaled Kim to silence the sounds of dozens of voices trying to speak with her at once. "Janeway to the fleet," she said, and felt as old as the prematurely aged ship when she spoke. "The Ammunii vessel was too close to a portal and was unable to alter course when it manifested. You have all seen the damage. There are no life signs. I can't explain it, not yet, but I don't want to lose anyone else. Please keep monitoring space. We will transmit what data we have as soon as we have it, but that wasn't enough to save the Ammunii. We will proceed forward in fifteen of our minutes. Stand by."

She sank back into her chair and closed her eyes for a moment.

"It wasn't your fault," said Chakotay, just loud enough for her to hear.

She opened her eyes and gazed at him. "Wasn't it? I'm the commander of this fleet."

"If this were normal space, I'm sure you'd emerge without a single ship lost," said Chakotay confidently. "But it isn't. We don't know yet how those things work. We can't predict when they will manifest. It wasn't your fault," he repeated.

On one level, she believed him. But on another level, she knew he was dead wrong.

The minutes ticked by as the straggling ships caught up to the main fleet. Janeway waited until the fifteen minutes had passed, then gave the order to proceed. But she did so with a heart that felt like lead in her chest.

"Do you now understand?" demanded Arkathi, from the privacy of his quarters.

"No one can predict these things," began Kelmar. Arkathi glowered at the ugly visage of the Iudka captain. Small, hairless, with glistening skin that reminded him of the unnatural glow of the V'enah skin. And those brightly colored clothes! Still, any ally would be welcome, even an ugly one.

"But they certainly made it seem as if they knew what they were doing, didn't they?" Arkathi persisted. "Almighty *Voyager*, we should be the flagship, we know all about the Alpha Quadrant. Pah! The Ammunii paid a deadly price for their blind trust."

Arkathi hadn't known which ship had gone through the deadly portal at the time. He had merely looked it up. He'd done his research since then, though.

"They were the right choice," Kelmar stubbornly persisted.

"I understand they're very friendly with your enemies," said Arkathi. "The Nenlar. They were the first people they found."

Kelmar stiffened. "We have no love for the Nenlar. They are cowards, even the bravest of them."

"Cowards need strong friends," said Arkathi. "Strong friends who can protect them from their enemies. Suppose Janeway knows exactly how these portals work and deliberately let the Ammunii wander into it."

Kelmar's face registered skepticism. "Highly unlikely."

"But it's possible. Anything is possible. Suppose they are even the ones controlling the portals? Suppose they are watching, waiting to pick us off one by one? The only ones who will make it across this so-called No Man's Land will be the ones that *Voyager* thinks will make good friends. You'll see."

"In that case," said Kelmar dryly, arching an eyebrow, "then I suspect we've seen the last of *you*."

The arrogance! Arkathi stifled the natural rage that surged up in him at the affront. Instead, he forced himself to chuckle, as if he and this disgusting humanoid were sharing a private joke.

"Witty as well as intelligent, I see," he said, while privately thinking nothing of the sort. "I ask nothing of you now."

"Which works well," said Kelmar, "as I intend to give you nothing."

"But keep your eyes open. Watch this Janeway closely. If it turns out they are trying to delude and betray us, then we would do well to have alliances among ourselves."

Kelmar did not reply. "Is this all, Arkathi?"

"All for now, my friend. Keep your eyes open." He severed the link before his ego got in the way of his ultimate plans. Out of the corner of his eye, he saw movement. He whirled quickly and snarled, "What are you doing here?"

Kella gasped and almost dropped the laden tray she bore. "You called me . . . asked me to prepare your meal . . ." she stammered.

Belatedly, he remembered she was right. He had forgotten. "What took you so long?" he snarled as she placed the tray down with hands that trembled. He wanted to ask her how much she had overheard. It was important that no one know that he was trying to stir up anti-*Voyager* sentiment. His plans would be much more effective if each group he spoke to thought they were the only ones.

"I know you don't like seeds in your fruits, and these were particularly seedy, so I—"

"Enough," he said, waving her out. She dropped

to her knees and bowed low before scurrying out as quickly as possible. As he chewed the juicy fruits, devoid of a single seed, he wondered if it was time to get a new personal servant and consign Kella to engineering. She had seen quite a bit.

Perhaps too much.

For a moment, Janeway's world went red. She held up a commanding hand and leaned forward intently into her viewscreen. "I certainly hope I misunderstood you, Leader Arkathi," she said, in a deceptively soft voice. "Do you mean to tell me that on an ordinary mission, the V'enah typically die? That you don't normally treat their injuries? What the hell *do* you do with them, let them lie where they fall and then just beam the bodies into space at your convenience?"

She'd intended the last sentence to be a horrendous overstatement, a ludicrous idea rife with angry sarcasm. But when Arkathi did not reply, Janeway realized with a frisson of horror that that was, indeed, precisely what the Todanians did.

"Oh my God," she breathed, suddenly cold. "What kind of monsters—"

"You asked us to join you, Janeway," hissed Arkathi. The sacs on his throat had inflated. He rose and, as Janeway was doing, leaned into the viewscreen. "We agreed. We thought you would help us, take care of us when we needed it. Protect us. Instead, you insult a way of life that has worked for us for centuries. You feed others, yet let my people go hungry. The V'enah are as much a part of this vessel as the engines, and while you happily replicate parts for other ships you deny us even medicines."

"Arkathi, please be silent." Stunned, he opened his mouth. "Listen to me. We will feed your people if they are hungry, but only if we are allowed to board your ship, distribute the food to *everyone,* and watch them eat. We will treat the injured, provided we can do so on site or that they beam aboard my ship and agree to have our doctor treat them in sickbay. I'll honor my part of the bargain. I'll help you and your people, *all* of them, survive No Man's Land." Again, he tried to interrupt. "No. I don't want to hear another word out of you. From here on in, any problems you have, you take them up with Commander Tuvok."

Furious, she switched off the viewscreen. Arkathi's ugly face disappeared. Breathing heavily, her face flushed, she strode onto the bridge.

"Captain, Leader Arkathi—" began Kim.

Janeway held up a hand to Kim and addressed Tuvok. "Tuvok. I need that calm, rational Vulcan manner of yours. I don't want to talk to Arkathi, not now, not in the foreseeable future. I'd like you to manage him for me."

Tuvok raised an eyebrow. "Of course, Captain. Mr. Kim, open the channel."

Janeway hastened back to the ready room before Tuvok could begin his conversation. She wasn't altogether surprised when, a few seconds later, Chakotay entered.

"What's happened now with our beloved Arkathi?" he asked.

The anger had faded somewhat, but not the righteous outrage. Janeway leaned back in her chair and sighed. "Same old song. But the treatment of the V'enah is worse than I imagined. They feed them only enough to keep them going, Chakotay. They don't 'waste' resources to heal them when they're injured. And when they die, as of course they must, apparently they just beam the bodies into space and pick up more. The V'enah are considered to be a disposable resource." The scorn dripped from her words.

Chakotay said nothing. A muscle tightened in his jaw, his handsome face reflecting her own horror. He offered no solution. He knew, as did she, that there really was none. And she was willing to bet that that thought rankled him every bit as much as it did her.

"He requested food and supplies," Janeway continued. "I told him that we'd bring the food over ourselves, and make sure everybody got to eat it. And if anyone's injured, they're to beam to our sickbay and the Doctor will tend to them. I'll be damned if I give them supplies that they hoard for use only on Todanians. The V'enah have to be treated and fed too."

"Good idea. I'll put Seven in charge of the away team."

"Seven? I was thinking that Neelix would be the logical choice."

"Under other conditions, I'd agree with you," Chakotay said. "But we're hardly trying to strike up a friendly relationship with the Todanians. It sounds like to me that you'd rather we concentrate on simply coexisting."

"You've got that right," said Janeway. She rose and went to the replicator. "Care for anything?"

"No, thank you."

"Coffee, black, hot." She indicated that he should continue while she sipped the steaming beverage.

"Seven has perhaps the closest comprehension of anyone aboard this ship of what it's like to be a slave. Drones are little more than a step up from slaves—or a step down, depending how you look at it. She's also a very keen observer and could get us some information about their vessel and its crew, just in case we needed it."

Janeway thought about it for a moment. "All right. I'll leave assembling the away team in your capable hands."

"I'll get right on it," Chakotay said. He turned to leave and almost collided with Tuvok.

"Captain," Tuvok said, stepping easily out of Chakotay's way, "I thought you might like to examine my conversation with Sinimar Arkathi."

She wrinkled her nose. "I wouldn't 'like' to have anything to do with Arkathi," she replied, even as she extended her hand for the padd.

"Perhaps I should rephrase my statement. I thought you would need to know what transpired during our conversation."

"Better," said Janeway, smiling. "Thanks, Tuvok." She heard the door hiss closed. She took another sip of coffee to brace herself, leaned back in her chair, and thumbed the controls.

Arkathi's visage was every bit as ugly in miniature as it was in real life, and his voice still grated.

"What . . . I demand to speak with Janeway!"

Tuvok's calm voice said, "Captain Janeway has left orders that you are to speak with me in all future conversations. You may either do so now, or not."

The red sacs inflated. "Very well." Janeway listened with half an ear to Arkathi's demands, and Tuvok's reasoned responses. She agreed with her chief of security on the amounts and types of food and care that would be provided, even as she thought that all this extra replicating was going to put a strain on the ship's resources. She'd hate to have to assign her own crew rations while the Todanians feasted.

Her full attention was seized a moment later. Arkathi, getting ready to sign off, seemingly couldn't let the conversation end without a parting shot.

"Your captain would do well to be more courteous, Commander."

"I have no reason to disapprove of my captain's behavior," Tuvok replied.

"You might regret those words."

"Explain."

"Let's just say that your high-handedness is not winning you many friends among this caravan. You and I have clashed openly, but there are others who are brooding in silence. You ought to watch your back, Tuvok. I'd be careful who I insulted if I were you."

Part of her wanted to dismiss this comment as more posturing by an arrogant, petty man. There was every reason to believe that Arkathi was making this up out of whole cloth.

But what if he wasn't? What if he was right? Mentally, she reviewed the various crews who had agreed to ally with her. The Hirogen, of course, were known enemies. There was an iciness between the Nenlar and the Iudka that could erupt into violence. They could have been lying, too, both races. Perhaps the Nenlar weren't as timid as they seemed, and perhaps the Iudka had never really abandoned their desire for conquest.

There were others, too, all of them unknown variables. She'd taken them on faith, and had asked the same courtesy of them. Everyone was going on trust.

What if that trust was misplaced?

She didn't want to go down that path. She was angry and stressed and, at least today, recognized when she needed a break. Returning the remaining portion of the coffee to the replicator, she strode onto the bridge and clapped a hand on Chakotay's shoulder.

"Stay there," she said, preventing him from rising from the captain's chair. "I'm going to sickbay."

Concern furrowed his face. "Are you not feeling well?"

"I'm all right. I just need some TLC therapy."

Now Chakotay looked puzzled and amused. "I know the Doctor has greatly improved his bedside manner, but I don't know that I'd go so far as to say he provides tender, loving care."

"That's not what it stands for," replied Janeway, grinning openly now. She headed for the turbolift, turned, and said, "It stands for tender, loving canine."

Janeway found Fluffy/Barkley chewing on the Doctor's boot. The hologram glanced up at her with an expression of long-suffering annoyance.

"Good morning, Captain." He rose and shook the animal loose from his boot. Barkley/Fluffy, tail wagging, clearly thought this was part of the game and joyously pounced on the boot again. "Is there something I can do for you?"

"You can let me take Fluffy off your hands—or at least your feet—for a while," Janeway replied.

His face lit up. "With pleasure," he said, and stooped to pick up the offending canine. "I suppose it's my own fault he's here," he said, scowling as the animal wriggled in his embrace and ecstatically licked his face with a black tongue. "Mr. Neelix wanted him in the mess hall, but I objected. A section of the ship where food is being prepared is no place for an animal. I suggested that Neelix confine Barkley to his quarters, but he got all upset. Said Fluffy—Barkley—whatever we're calling him today—would get lonely, and that since I had forbidden him from the mess hall, I could jolly well look after him in sickbay."

"And Neelix was right," stated Janeway, gathering the dog into her arms. A wave of affection washed over her. It had been so long since she had cradled a small animal in her arms. It wasn't quite a dog, no, but it was close enough. Barkley/Fluffy was warm, and affectionate, and Janeway felt a quiet joy steal over her. Oh, she had missed this, the purity of the interaction between human and mute beast. She was glad Neelix had protested her leaving Barkley/Fluffy on the planet. He was right. The animal would have died. And she would not have had this chance to experience the happy bond between them as she was doing right now.

"Yes, you're a good boy, aren't you?" she said to him. He wriggled with pleasure, and she laughed. Looking up, she laughed again at the expression on the Doctor's face. "You've never known the joys of pet ownership."

"On the contrary," said the Doctor. "I've had two sets of boots ruined and have had to clean up several messes."

"First thing on the agenda, then," said Janeway, "is to get this little fellow housebroken."

"Hallelujah," said the Doctor, dryly.

"Seriously," continued Janeway, strangely anxious to get the Doctor's approval of the creature, "it's been documented that simply stroking a pet lowers human blood pressure. Pets are very healthy."

"Then why aren't they standard issue aboard a starship?" retorted the Doctor.

She gave him a broad smile. "You know, I've no idea. Maybe it's something we need to take up with Starfleet Command once we get home." Janeway winked. "Come on, Fluffy. Or Barkley. You've got some tricks to learn."

She allotted herself twenty minutes to begin teaching Barkley/Fluffy some basic obedience commands. Janeway had trained many dogs over the years, but she was amazed at how quickly this one picked up the instructions. By the end of twenty minutes, he had mastered "sit," "stay," "come," "down," and "heel."

"What a good dog!" she enthused, and Fluffy/Barkley wriggled with pleasure. She was on her knees, rubbing his belly enthusiastically while his tail thumped the floor of the holodeck, when her combadge chirped.

"Chakotay to Janeway."

She sighed. "What is it, Commander? And please don't tell me it's our friend Arkathi again."

"No, someone else. I hate to interrupt your tender, loving canine therapy, but I think you'd better get up to the bridge."

She looked down at Barkley/Fluffy, who had frozen and was staring at her with those enormous slitted eyes. It was as if he was afraid that if he moved, she wouldn't resume petting him. Janeway gave his stomach a final rub, then stood up. Immediately Barkley/Fluffy scrambled into a sitting position, awaiting her next command.

"Very well. Let me take my therapist back to sickbay and I'll be right there."

"I don't understand it myself," Commander Ellia said, twining her first set of paws together in what was clearly agitation. Her large, fawn-colored ears flapped. "It's quite embarrassing. You've done so much for our ship, and you haven't accepted anything in return. We really don't feel we can impose upon you further, but. . . ." She opened both sets of forelegs in a helpless gesture. "We have to keep up with you. There's really nothing for it. Perhaps some of our delicacies? We know that you have a replicator and it's not necessary, but we'd feel better if you take *something*."

Species like the Salamar, with the polite, friendly Commander Ellia as their spokesperson, were what kept Janeway from feeling complete cynicism on this strange mission. They were a pleasant, advanced species, whose entire social structure centered around the concept of fairness, balance, and equity. After her dealing with Arkathi, such a race was almost a dream come true for Janeway. They had been unwilling to accept, as a gift, the offer of *Voyager*'s protection and guidance at first. Finally, Janeway had talked them into it, saying that she was certain there would come a time when a fair trade would be negotiated. This had mollified Ellia somewhat, and until now, Janeway had heard nothing more from the *Umul*.

But now, Ellia had contacted Janeway and explained that, for some reason, the *Umul* was being drained of power. If it continued, they would no longer be able to keep up with the caravan without being towed.

"I'll send my chief engineer and a team to take a look for you," Janeway reassured the alien commander. "And yes, we will take any offers of food you can provide. It seems that there are many in the caravan who are running out of supplies, and I'm not sure we can replicate enough food for everyone."

Ellia wrinkled her long, flexible, black nose. "I'm relieved to hear that, Captain. Not of course that there is a food shortage, but that you are finally willing to accept a trade for your services. Your chief engineer will be a welcome figure on our ship, believe me. Thank you."

"My pleasure," said Janeway, and meant it. When the image of Ellia blinked out, she wondered why everyone couldn't be as pleasant a traveling companion as Ellia.

"Bridge to engineering."

"Go ahead, Captain," came Torres's voice.

"I know you've got your hands full, but could you spare the time to take a look at the Salamar ship? They're reporting an unknown power drain."

"You're kidding."

"I'd hardly joke about something so serious," said Janeway. "Why? What's going on?"

"Well, I've been talking to the chief engineers on some of the other ships, and two of them have reported a similar problem."

Chakotay, who had been listening quietly, offered, "That's not good."

It most certainly wasn't. "Torres, I want you to do a full level-one diagnostic on the warp core and the engines. We can only help others if we make sure that we ourselves aren't in trouble. After that, I want you to take a team over to the *Umul* and see if you can't figure out what's going on."

"I'll get right on it, Captain. Torres out."

"One ship having a mysterious power drain is a problem, but it can be remedied," said Chakotay. "But three ships, all completely different in design, but all with the same problem—that can't be a coincidence."

"I'm certain it's not," said Janeway. "We'll have to find out what these three disparate ships have in common, besides going through a gateway."

"Maybe they went through the same gateway," offered Chakotay.

"Or perhaps," said Janeway, with growing unease, "simply going through a gateway at all did the trick."

Chakotay grimaced. "I don't like where that train of thought is heading."

"Neither do I," said Janeway, "but we've got to investigate all possibilities."

CHAPTER

9

SEVEN OF NINE WAS IRKED. IT WAS A TERM SHE HAD just learned from the Doctor a short time ago, and she found it to be an apt one for describing the nuances of this particular emotion. She was not upset enough to be irritated, and certainly was not angry. "Vexed," another term to which the Doctor had introduced her, might also apply. But she thought she'd continue with "irked."

She was irked because Chakotay had made it clear that they were not only to offer food and medical aid to the Todanians and the V'enah, but were also to "keep an eye out for anything that might be useful." Seven knew that Chakotay's euphemism translated into "spy." She was to observe and report back. But Sinimar Arkathi had preempted any reconnaissance she might attempt. He had isolated Seven and the

Doctor in a single large room, and told her that he would send in his crew in small groups. Four guards stood beside the single door, holding weapons and looking menacing. Seven had already thoroughly examined this room, and it was comparable to a cargo bay aboard *Voyager*. She would learn nothing helpful here.

She decided to turn her attention to learning what she could about the Todanians and V'enah instead. They prepared the rations; then Arkathi let his people enter in groups of ten at a time.

"Please line up in single file," Seven said. "You may approach the Doctor first, and then I will give you your meal."

"One meal?" cried Arkathi. "We have hungry people aboard this ship. I expected at least a few days' worth of rations. Your captain is a stingy woman."

Seven turned to face him. "My captain fears that the Todanians will hoard the food and supplies," she said bluntly. She saw no reason for politeness or subterfuge. "She is worried that Todanians will be treated and fed, and that the V'enah will not. The only way to ensure that all aboard your vessel receive equal treatment is for us to feed and treat each individual, one at a time." She turned to a stack of boxes.

Arkathi stormed over to her. "You can't do this."

She straightened and looked him directly in the eye. "It is either this way, or no one aboard this ship will receive food or medical treatment. It is immaterial to me which. I have duties aboard my ship. What do you wish?"

Janeway had told Seven that when he became agitated, Arkathi had sacs on either side of his neck that inflated and turned red. She watched, mildly interested in the phenomenon, as they did so now. Without another word, he stalked out.

"Good," said the Doctor. "It'll be easier without him hovering." He turned to the first Todanian, who was shifting uneasily and glancing at the guards, and smiled broadly. "No need to be worried. I'm just going to scan you to see if you need medical treatment. I'll treat you here if I can, and if not, then you get a special trip to *Voyager's* sickbay."

He scanned the Todanian. "Mild dehydration," he said, to no one in particular. He applied a hypo and admonished, "Keep drinking your water, good fellow," then turned to the next alien in line.

Seven handed the Todanian a box. "I understand that your people eat only once in a twenty-four-hour cycle. This contains sufficient rations for one full day. Sit out of our way and consume it." She pointed to the far end of the large, square room.

The Todanian glared at her. She frowned. "Comply."

Muttering under his breath, he did so. The next Todanian in line seemed much happier to be there than either Arkathi or the first to receive treatment.

"You are kind to help us," he said to the Doctor.

The Doctor raised an eyebrow. Seven supposed that he, as she was, was surprised by the polite words and tone of voice.

"You're welcome," said the Doctor. "I'm sorry it's necessary to treat you like you are hoarding thieves, but your captain has made behaving otherwise impossible."

The Todanian seemed to want to say something more, but glanced over at the four guards and was silent. Seven handed him his rations. He nodded, hesitated, then walked over to join his crewmate.

For the most part, they were sullenly silent, though some appeared to be more personable than others. No one rivaled his commander for outrage and arrogance, for which Seven was grateful. The guards were bristlingly attentive at first, then gradually seemed to grow bored. They lowered their weapons and began to talk among themselves.

She was not learning much, and she would have preferred to be at her post in astrometrics. The caravan was traveling through dangerous territory. Seven knew she would be of more use back on *Voyager.* Anyone could perform the task here.

Finally, they had gone through the Todanian crew. As the last few left, one of them turned. "The V'enah will be sent in shortly," he said.

They were left alone. The Doctor sighed. "Let me guess, Seven. You feel like your time and unique talents are being wasted on this assignment."

"Correct," said Seven.

"So do I. Anyone could administer these vitamin supplements and rehydration hypos. I haven't even seen so much as a scratch on any of them. The Todanians are almost obscenely healthy. Some of them," he added archly, "could stand to skip a few meals."

Seven had had enough. She touched her combadge. "Seven of Nine to Commander Chakotay." She didn't want to talk to Janeway. Chakotay was the one who had somehow decided that she would be right for this mission; Chakotay was the one she'd complain to.

"This is Chakotay. How's it going?"

"Inefficiently," Seven replied. "They have isolated

us in a cargo bay and are sending the Todanians in for treatment and food. I request to be relieved of this assignment."

"Me too," said the Doctor.

"As does the Doctor. There's nothing—"

The door hissed open, the guards straightened, and Seven paused in midsentence, her attention utterly seized.

Ten figures entered the room. They did not stride in like the Todanians. They moved stiffly, their eyes downcast. Some clutched their arms or sides. Others limped, or were assisted by their companions. Through the skintight, torn, filthy jumpsuits they wore, Seven could see ribs.

A woman brought up their rear. At first glance, there was nothing extraordinary about her. She stumbled in, her eyes on the floor, like all the rest. But for one instant, while the guards' attention was diverted to others, her head came up and her eyes met those of Seven evenly. And Seven of Nine, who had seen much and learned more, felt as though a phaser blast had struck her.

The woman was tall and almost painfully thin. Her hair was cropped close to her skull. It looked like she had cut it herself. She was, as were all the V'enah, a peculiar combination of muscles and wasted flesh. There was no fat to soften the angles of her face and body, only knotted muscle, sinew, and bone.

Slaves. The captain had told Seven that the V'enah were slaves of the Todanians. The word had a companion in Seven's mind: drone. Except these people were cognizant of everything they were being made to do. There was no pacifier to their servitude, no sense of "serving the collective." They were individuals, were abused as individuals, suffered as individuals. She did not know if the Todanians were kind masters, but she could make an educated guess by looking at the gaunt bodies, the haunted expressions, the scars and injuries on the pale purple flesh.

A wave of righteous anger swept through Seven's body as she continued to lock gazes with the woman. A word popped into her brain, though she did not intentionally summon it:

Sister.

Seven of Nine had had no sister, no siblings at all. But she had educated herself on the matter of family relations, and understood the concept. This woman, though they had never met before and were not even of the same species, was closer kin to Seven than the parents she dimly remembered. They were alike in their suffering, and in their will to be unconquered.

At that moment, Seven had two impulses. The first was to revert to her Borg socialization, to impartially classify these people and coolly analyze their plight. The second one surprised her, for it chased away that deep-seated reaction and supplanted it with another, more human one: she realized that she was going to do everything in her power to free these people. She recognized the thought as illogical, impractical, and possibly insane. But it gripped her with talons of steel and would not be denied.

"My God," said the Doctor. "Doctor to Lieutenant Paris. If the captain can spare you, I need you to report to sickbay immediately. Prepare to receive several patients for treatment. Possibly emergency."

"Understood, Doctor. Captain says I'm on my way."

The Doctor's words broke the spell the woman's purple gaze had cast upon Seven. She inhaled swiftly and realized that for the last several seconds she hadn't been breathing. Her heart was racing and she recognized the stinging in her eyes as a passionate desire to weep. Remarkable. With deliberation, she placed the mask of cool competence on her face. Her wailing and empathy would be of no use to these people. Feeding them and healing their injuries would be.

"All of you, sit down at once. Lie as still as possible until I have a chance to ascertain the extent of your injuries," ordered the Doctor.

The V'enah, almost as one, shrank from the briskness of his tone. As if on cue, the guards marched up to the small group and closed in around them. One of them raised his weapon and, before either Seven or the Doctor could react, slammed the butt of it into a V'enah's shoulder.

"Drop, vermin! You will obey orders!"

He raised the weapon again, but this time, Seven was there. She interposed her body between the guard and the cringing V'enah and, more quickly than the shocked guard could react, struck his arm and pulled it behind his back. The weapon clattered to the floor. At once, Seven released the guard.

"You will cease injuring the V'enah," she ordered. "You will cease interfering with the job we were sent to do and resume your posts at the door."

The unfortunate guard who had borne the brunt of her wrath rubbed his aching arm, then retrieved his weapon. His companion snarled, "We don't take orders from you."

"Then our mission here is completed, and your captain will be . . . irked."

Now the guard looked uncomfortable. They exchanged glances, then, without another word, stomped back to their original positions. They glowered, but Seven was not ruffled. She returned her attention to the V'enah. The Doctor was already treating the one who had been struck, and several of them looked to the one woman who had so captivated Seven of Nine. She nodded.

"They are here to help us," she said. Her voice was husky, both gentle and strong at the same time, pitched just softly enough so that the guards would not hear. "Do what they tell you to."

At her words, they nodded and got to the floor. Some of them hissed in pain at the movements. The Doctor literally tossed the medical tricorder to Seven of Nine while he gathered his tools. Seven went straight to the woman who seemed to be their leader and began to scan her.

A purple hand closed on her arm. "No," said the woman. "There are others who need your care first."

"You all need our care," stated Seven, trying to keep her voice from trembling. "They seem to listen to you. Tell me about them."

"There is little to tell," said the woman as Seven scanned her. "We are the V'enah. We are bred to be slaves to the Todanians. We are disposable."

Seven recognized that the woman was trying to sound submissive, but failing. She guessed that the woman did not have much interaction with the Todanians personally, wherever she was stationed. They would have crushed that fiery rebellion inside her long before now, or else killed her in the process.

"What is your designation?"

"My what?"

"Your name."

"It is of no consequence."

"What is your name?" Seven repeated.

"Marisha," the woman replied. Then, almost shyly, "What is yours?"

"I am Seven of Nine. It is a Borg designation."

"I do not know the Borg. Not that we are permitted interaction with other species. Only the personal slaves do that."

Seven turned toward the Doctor. "Minor dermal abrasions. One recent, severe burn on the hand. It has been tended to, but inefficiently. Several old scars. Dehydration and malnutrition, which will probably be standard among the V'enah. If you will hand me the dermal regenerator, I can begin treatment."

The Doctor did so, exchanging the regenerator for the medical tricorder. He bent down beside one of the sicker V'enah and ran the tricorder over his body.

"Paris to the Doctor. I'm in sickbay and ready to handle the patients."

"Excellent," said the Doctor. "I'm sending you four right now. I'll stay here and keep tending the rest. And Mr. Paris?"

"Yeah, Doc?"

"This is only the first group."

A pause, then, "Understood." The Doctor stepped back, and four of the most seriously injured V'enah dematerialized.

Seven returned her attention to Marisha. "Extend your hand."

Marisha did so, bright purple eyes taking in everything. "Dermal regenerator," she said. "Dermal meaning skin, regenerator meaning re-create. Is that correct?"

"Essentially," said Seven, running the warm red light over Marisha's swollen, injured hand and taking a keen pleasure in watching the injury vanish.

Marisha gaped openly. "This is . . . this is amazing!" She touched her formerly injured hand with the other one. "No more pain, no swelling. . . ."

"This is the least of our medical treatments," said Seven. "Rest assured that your people will be well by the time they return to their posts."

"Posts," repeated Marisha. "As if we had posts as the Todanians do. We have sections. We stay in that section until we die. Your treatments are welcome, Seven of Nine, but they are only temporary. This hand will likely be burned again by tomorrow."

Seven of Nine swallowed, but continued treating Marisha. "What is your section?" she asked, placing the first hypo on Marisha's long, pale purple throat and pressing gently.

Over the hiss of the hypo, Marisha replied, "Engineering. We operate the heavy machinery. It is one of the more dangerous tasks aboard the ship."

Seven nodded to herself. She had been correct. If it was a dangerous task, it would not be likely that there would be many Todanians involved. Marisha indeed did not have much day-to-day contact with her . . . her owners.

She wished to continue conversing with Marisha,

but had finished treating her. Reluctantly, Seven pointed the other woman toward the large pile of boxed rations. "Each box contains a full day's rations, to be consumed here, in our presence."

Marisha studied Seven of Nine intently, then nodded. "I understand," she said, softly. "You do not think the Todanians will give us the food if you are not here to watch us eat it."

"Correct."

A sad smile curved Marisha's full mouth. "You are right. They would save it for themselves. I thank you." She took one of the boxes and sat down. After opening it, she stared at the contents.

"Is something wrong?" asked Seven.

"Nothing," said Marisha. "I . . . I have never seen so much food in my life. I hardly know where to begin."

Seven raised an eyebrow, even as she knelt beside another V'enah and administered a hypo for rehydration. "Select a food item and eat it," she offered.

Marisha laughed. It was deep and warm and rumbling. "I suppose you're right."

"There is not that much," said Seven, continuing to treat the other V'enah. "According to our estimates, that is the standard amount of calories and nutrients you should be consuming per day."

"We get about a third of this," said the woman Seven was treating. Seven glanced down at her. She was pretty, dressed in a flowing, attractive garment with her long, dark purple hair piled decoratively atop her head. She was nowhere near as gaunt or haggard-looking as most of her companions. "I get more. Arkathi gives it to me and I steal what he does not eat off his plate."

"You serve Arkathi?" asked Seven.

"I am his personal servant. I am Kella." She bit her lip and looked down. "I have not seen the others before now. I didn't know how badly . . . Are you done?"

"Yes," Seven said, looking shrewdly at Kella. The serving girl rose, grabbed a box, looked over apprehensively at the guards, and headed for a corner where she could be alone to wolf down the food.

"Seven," said the Doctor, motioning her to attend him. She knelt by his side, utilizing the dermal regenerator on a male V'enah who had severe lacerations on his back. "Don't tell me, let me guess," he said, glancing up at Marisha, who had followed Seven. "This gentleman misbehaved."

"I was wrong," grunted the man. Seven stared at the wounds, barely crusted over and oozing pus. They vanished beneath the warm, red light. Seven had never felt so good about medical technology before, not even when she was the recipient of its wonders. "I disobeyed. . . ."

"Talyk, you did nothing wrong!" Marisha knelt beside his head and touched his hair gently. "You had never been in that part of the ship before and you were following orders. It wasn't your fault you got lost."

"This man was beaten because he took an incorrect turn in your ship?" Seven asked, incredulous. Marisha nodded. "Your collective is unhealthy and dangerous. You should leave it."

"Seven," cautioned the Doctor. "That's not our place."

"It is not our place to stop a vicious injustice?"

Seven demanded. "Slavery is a cruel, inhumane, and impractical institution. It should be opposed whenever we encounter it. I know you, Doctor, and I know that you agree with me."

Marisha's wide eyes were glued on Seven. Her breasts rose and fell with rapid, shallow breathing.

The Doctor rose. "Come with me," he said. Still raging inside, Seven complied. When they were out of earshot of the Todanians, the Doctor hissed, "Of course I abhor slavery! But that's not the point."

"Standing up for what is right is not the point?"

"You are twisting my words. You know exactly what I mean. This is not the time or place to stage a revolution. We are traveling through a very treacherous part of space. We have struck up an agreement that is tenuous at best with a species that still doesn't trust us. Our job is to get everyone, including the Todanians, safely through No Man's Land. And our immediate job is to provide care and food for everyone, including the Todanians, aboard this ship. Is that clear?"

"Perfectly," she said, and she saw him flinch at the iciness of her tone.

"You are free to make a detailed report to Captain Janeway. And we both know she'll listen to what you have to say with a sympathetic ear. Maybe when this is all over, we can help the V'enah with more than medical treatment and rations, but for now, we have to remain calm. Don't fan the fires, Seven. Not now, not yet."

They returned to the V'enah. Seven did not trust herself to speak and turned away from Marisha, ostensibly to aid the Doctor. But despite her feigned nonchalance, Seven was acutely aware of the other woman's presence, of the glowering, hostile presence of the only temporarily cowed guards, of the timid, well-treated Kella cowering alone in the corner, and of the unjustness of the wounded whom they were treating; healing, only to be injured again.

CHAPTER
10

TORRES WAS IN HEAVEN. WELL, AS CLOSE TO HEAVEN as she was going to get in this lifetime, anyway.

Neelix, bless him, had come up with a brilliant idea. They had been only three days into the territory called No Man's Land and things were already starting to get bad. They lost that first ship, the Ammunii, just a couple of hours in, and that had brought everything to a screeching halt. Another meeting was held, and the fleet finally began to move on. They were stopped again almost immediately by the unexpected violence of the first official obstacle, an asteroid belt composed of asteroids so comparatively tiny and crowded together so densely that some of the smaller vessels whose shields weren't as powerful as *Voyager*'s would be at risk.

Torres was itching to move more quickly, to put

this treacherous area of space and its tensions behind them, but Janeway had stated quite firmly that they could move no faster than the slowest vessels. And some of those vessels were damn slow. What was worse, more and more of them seemed to be experiencing the peculiar power drain. Torres was getting frustrated at having to continue working on a puzzle she got no closer to solving.

Torres knew in her gut that this couldn't continue. So when Neelix had made his brilliant suggestion, she wanted to throw her arms around his stocky frame and kiss him.

"Why don't we have an exchange program?" he had said his chipper voice. "We could have some individuals from these other ships visit *Voyager* and learn about our technology and cultures, and we could visit them. I'd love to have someone to swap recipes with. I can't wait to share my secrets for making the perfect *leola*-root stew!" He had actually rubbed his hands together in anticipation.

B'Elanna met Tom's eyes, and saw her own excitement reflected there. At the same time, they said, "Ask the captain."

He had asked, she had (according to Neelix) agreed before he had even finished articulating the idea, and things were being put in motion even as Torres lay beneath a console, tinkering with a faulty connection. Apparently, the crews of the other vessels were as screamingly bored as she was.

Yesterday was the first exchange. Since the plan had been Neelix's idea, his request had been the first granted. Six aliens, none of whom was familiar and all of whom were unfailingly polite, had congregated in the mess hall to learn the mysteries of *leola*-root stew, coffee substitutes, and *yruss*-and-broccoli. It seemed as though everyone on board the ship needed a snack at one point during the day. Torres herself, claiming a desire for some fresh fruit, had wandered in and had barely restrained herself from laughing with delight.

Neelix looked ecstatic, clad from head to toe in full chef's regalia. Staring at him solemnly, almost worshipfully, were the six aliens. Three were humanoid, two were bipedal but resembled birds and lizards more than humans, and one was a small sphere that hovered by itself and occasionally extended a digit or two to assist with the preparation of a chocolate soufflé. Ironically, despite the notorious difficulty of preparing a soufflé from scratch and how poor his cooking sometimes was, Neelix was always very good at this, and it never failed to impress. Even as Torres watched, munching on an apple, Neelix drew the treat out of the oven to a soft chorus of oohs and aahs.

She grinned now at the memory, finished her task, and scooted out from under the console. "Another hour and they'll be here," she said enthusiastically to Vorik.

He favored her with a brief glance, then returned to his padd. "We have been prepared for them since 0700 hours," he said calmly. "There is nothing to worry about."

"I'm not worried, I'm excited," said Torres. "It's something to break the tension. And it could be fun."

"I am experiencing neither tension nor excitement, Lieutenant, as you well know. And fun is irrelevant."

122

"Now you're starting to sound like Seven," chided Torres. "You have to admit, it will be a fascinating experience to have so many diverse races the Federation has never before encountered on this ship, in engineering."

He paused and considered the question seriously. "It will indeed be educational," he finally said.

Torres rolled her eyes. Vulcans.

"Vulcans," sighed Janeway. Tuvok raised an eyebrow at her exasperation. "Why didn't you mention this before?"

"I was not aware of it before," said Tuvok, as if it was the most logical thing in the world, which of course it was. "It was only this morning that the Doctor informed me of Mr. Neelix's food-poisoning incident."

Janeway had just returned from the Doctor. It had not been a pleasant encounter. Apparently, chocolate was quite toxic to one of the races who had sampled the soufflé and the alien had almost died. They had sent a note to the Doctor, not Janeway, and it was almost apologetic in tone. When Janeway read it, despite the seriousness of the situation, she'd practically laughed out loud. The Lamorians were most embarrassed, but they felt it necessary to report that one of their number had taken a bit ill, well, almost died, truth be told, from something in Mr. Neelix's delicious, exquisite soufflé, and they felt that it was incumbent on them to alert the Doctor to this fact, just in case some other alien might have reacted similarly and might need treatment, though the soufflé was most wonderful and Mr. Neelix was obviously a man greatly skilled at his craft and . . .

"Captain, I'm simply mortified," said Neelix, and it was obvious from his expression that he was not exaggerating. "I sent a list to all the ships with the chemical composition of all the foods we'd be eating, and no one said a thing!"

"Apparently in Lamorian society, it is the host's duty to never serve anything harmful," said the Doctor. "Though how one is expected to do that when an alien's body chemistry is unfamiliar I'm sure I don't know. As far as they were concerned, it was a terrible social blunder on our part and they didn't want to cause us to lose face."

"I'd rather lose face than be inadvertently responsible for a lost life," said Janeway. "Let's hope they'll be a little more forthcoming in the future."

And now, Tuvok was standing in front of her insisting that they cancel the exchange program. "It was a misunderstanding about food, Tuvok," said Janeway. "It's unlikely to happen again. Everyone here knows the common language of engineering or piloting—"

"Commander Chakotay has offered to have a ritual ceremony," said Tuvok stubbornly. "Suppose someone has a moral objection to an object utilized in the ritual? Suppose Mr. Paris's friendly game of pool results in an injury?"

"Careful, kid, you'll poke your eye out," muttered Paris from the conn.

"Tuvok, those are culture clashes that happen every day," began Janeway, but Tuvok wouldn't let it go.

"There is also the very real risk of injury to members of our own crew aboard the alien vessels. I was uneasy with this idea to begin with, but I understand the necessity for keeping morale high while traversing a dangerous stretch of space, especially in the company of so many alien ships. However, after the chocolate incident, it is my considered opinion that we should terminate these programs at once."

"You're an excellent security chief, Tuvok," Janeway said sincerely. "But I'm the captain, and it is *my* considered opinion that the good to be obtained from these exchanges far outweighs any risk. This is an unprecedented opportunity to learn so much from so many races in this comparatively short time, and I won't miss it. We'll proceed as planned."

If Vulcans could glower, Tuvok would have done so. Instead, he contented himself with a raised eyebrow and returned to his post. He'd known her long enough to know when argument was useless.

Word spreads fast on a starship, and it wasn't long before everyone knew about the Chocolate Incident, as it came to be called. Torres heard about it right before the doors hissed open and an amazing collection of aliens poured into engineering. She was certain that at any minute her combadge was going to spring to life with Janeway's voice ordering an immediate termination of the exchange program, or else Tuvok and his security guards were going to burst in. Consequently, with this weighing heavily on her mind, she didn't have as wonderful a time as she had hoped. Nonetheless, by the time she'd escorted the group of seventeen around engineering, had them try out a few things themselves, and learned about two entirely new ways of traversing space at faster-than-light speed, she was still having a pretty darned good time.

It was about then when one of the aliens bumped, struck, or otherwise accidentally managed to rupture a plasma conduit.

"Who was it?" Tom asked later, over chicken sandwiches and tomato soup.

"I never did find out in the ensuing chaos," said Torres, biting savagely into the sandwich. "Apparently the Kuluuk are extremely timid. A good scare can literally kill them."

"I'd say that a plasma conduit venting gas in an enclosed space is a good scare," said Tom.

"You're telling me. Not only did we have to completely evacuate engineering, we had to rush the Kuluuk to sickbay, their little green, furry faces all tight with terror and their paws waving in the air—" She shuddered. "You wonder how a species that vulnerable ever made it into space."

"So how did they?"

Torres shrugged. "I didn't pay that much attention to their bios. Something about how they were the darlings of some incredibly tolerant empire who protected them, sent them on non-dangerous missions for the good of the empire. Can't blame that empire; they're cute little guys and very sweet-natured. Fortunately, only two of their hearts had stopped, and the Doc was able to give them a sedative that prevented them from going into a fatal shock. But it was close, Tom."

"So, we've got the Chocolate Incident and the

Warp Core Near Catastrophe. Can't wait to see what will happen tomorrow."

"What's tomorrow?" Torres spooned up a mouthful of soup.

"Piloting," said Tom. "My turn to have an incident."

Neelix had stopped by to pour them each more coffee substitute. "I'd avoid another incident if I were you," he said. "Mr. Vulcan is on the warpath. He's just looking for a reason to cancel this exchange program." The Talaxian sighed heavily. "I certainly did my share to jeopardize it."

"You've got company," Torres offered reassuringly. "Don't blow it for everyone else, Tom."

"Oh, thanks. No pressure at all, is there?"

"Obstacle number two," said Janeway, more to herself than Seven as they stood together in astrometrics.

"Correct," said Seven, "out of approximately thirty-three, based on my present calculations. That is not including the continued manifestations of the gateways."

Janeway hadn't needed to hear that. "We'll take them one at a time." She stepped forward, tapped the controls, and read the information. "Hmm. Sounds like the Mutara Nebula. Just what we need with thirty-two ships in tow."

"I am not familiar with the Mutara Nebula."

"No, you wouldn't be." Janeway gazed at the screen. There, the nebula was just an icon of yellow swirls. In reality, it would be something much more beautiful, mysterious—and dangerous. "Back in the twenty-third century, Admiral James T. Kirk utilized the Mutara Nebula, one similar to this, but much smaller, in which to hide from the pursuer Khan Noonien Singh."

Seven frowned. "From what I have learned of Admiral Kirk, he would not have favored hiding as a tactic."

"He would if it enabled him to get the jump on his adversary, which it did. For us, though, it's nothing but an enormous headache. This class of nebula wreaks havoc with the sensors. We won't be able to see past a few thousand meters, we won't have shields or sensors or probably even standard lighting. Let's see if we can't just go around it."

"Inadvisable. The area is several million kilometers in diameter. Also, we would be encountering the residue of the asteroid belt—"

"—which already cost us at least one vessel," Janeway finished. She sighed, heavily. "We can do it, but it's not going to be easy."

"I do not believe we expected any part of this journey to be easy," Seven reminded her.

"No, but anything in the vicinity of slightly-less-than-almost-impossible would be quite welcome along about now."

"Only seventeen ships gave us sufficient details about their vessels for us to determine if they can make it through safely," Torres grumbled at the senior staff meeting a half hour later. "The rest still don't trust us enough."

"That's regrettable," said Janeway, "but it's not altogether surprising. It's an extremely unusual situation for all of us, and if the shoe was on the other foot I'm not sure I'd give up important information like that too readily. We'll just have to give them the information we have about the nebula and trust them to make the judgment. In the meantime, here's what we've got."

She thumbed a control and various statistics appeared on the screen. "There are a couple of ships who might be technologically superior to *Voyager.* As Lieutenant Torres has said, we don't know for certain. There are several ships that we know are comparable to ours, and more than that which are inferior. These would be the smaller, scout-type ships, by and large. The Nenlar vessel, for example. We know that once we enter the nebula, all our bells and whistles won't make that much difference. It's *Voyager's* bulk and the experience of her crew that is going to be key. Since we're leading this rather odd mission, we go through first."

She paused, and looked at her officers. "Anyone ever traversed one of these before?" No one replied. "Me either. But from what I understand, we'll be flying blind. We'll have to go on impulse power for certain. We'll have no sensors, no shields, no visual except for very short distances, and it'll be erratic at that. We might have a tractor beam, but it's iffy and it would degrade the farther away the towed object is from the ship."

"I'm not personally familiar with this type of nebula," said Chakotay, "but from what I remember of the Badlands, I'm betting it's likely that it won't be a straight shot through, either."

"Correct," said Seven. "Preliminary research and sensor findings indicate that there are a variety of eddies and other phenomena within the nebula. It is impossible to chart a path through without actually experiencing it. It is also highly likely that these eddies and rifts would be subject to extreme fluctuation."

"So here's my plan," said Janeway. "*Voyager* goes through first. The sensors won't work, we're fairly certain of that. But it's likely we'll have some visual, though it'll be poor. How are your eyes, Mr. Paris?"

"Been eating my carrots, ma'am," Paris replied.

She smiled. "Good. Because visual is going to be all we've got. We'll talk to the captains of each ship and have them give me their best guess as to how far they'll be able to see. Some won't be able to see at all. What we'll do is, every few hundred kilometers, more often if need be, we'll drop a probe modified to serve as a beacon. Torres tells me it should work. I understand there are certain frequencies that can penetrate this nebula. We'll just have to experiment until we find it. We'll leave the beacons at regular intervals, more often around dangerous areas; then we'll have the ships go through one at a time."

"I would recommend having a predetermined order," said Tuvok. "And having each ship depart at a precise time. We must proceed carefully and slowly. If even one ship misses a buoy, or for any reason fails to navigate the course properly, or succumbs to the power drain several ships are still experiencing, we will have to perform a rescue mission."

"Which will be like trying to find a needle in a haystack," said Kim morosely.

"We'll do everything we can to avoid that, of course," said Janeway, "but I want it understood that

that's a possibility. No ship will be left behind, no matter what it takes."

About two hours later, Janeway rubbed her temple. Tension headache. Again. The Doctor would be quite vexed with her.

It had sounded so easy, so logical, with her own staff in the briefing room. It made perfect sense. But now that she was having to discuss it with each race, one by one, all with their own opinions and problems, she was beginning to think it would all have been so much easier had she simply gone around the nebula.

The Lamorians had a religious problem. Nebulas were holy places to them. They never entered them; it was where their gods dwelt. Janeway had sent Chakotay over to their ship to discuss it with them. If anyone could convince them that their gods would rather they pay them a visit than die lost in space, it was he. She hadn't heard from him, but she hoped for the best.

The Nenlars had objected to what, to them, amounted to "being alone in a dark room with our deadliest enemies." The Iudka had scornfully replied that if they had any designs on the Nenlars, they'd have blasted their pathetic little ship out of space long before now.

The Iyal were more than willing, but only if they could lead. The Tllihuh also were amenable, but they wanted to be able to determine the order. The Hirogen had agreed, almost too quickly. Janeway didn't want to look a gift horse in the mouth, but their quick acquiescence was bothering her. The Yumiri would go, but only after some elaborate ritual involving honoring every crewman's ancestors to the tenth degree. Janeway suggested that they hop right on it.

And on and on it went. Two ships flatly refused and departed. Janeway couldn't honestly say she was sorry to see them go. The fewer voices there were raised in protest of every decision she made, the easier it was.

Some of the aliens had genuine complaints. One group's technology was so far behind that the ionized gases of the nebula would stop it dead in its tracks. It wouldn't be able to move at all under its own power. Fortunately, another ship agreed to tow the smaller one, without any additional encouragement from Janeway at all. Still others would be completely blinded and also require a tractor beam from a larger, benevolent vessel.

At one point, her combadge chirped. "Chakotay to bridge."

"Janeway here. Go ahead."

"The Lamorians have agreed to enter the nebula—on one condition."

"They've got it."

"That I stay on their ship for the duration of the trip."

Damn, Janeway thought. "For what reason?"

"I appear to have made quite an impression on them. They seem to think that I have some kind of pull with their gods."

"Well, I knew you had clout, Chakotay, but I never dreamed," said Janeway, fighting back a smile.

"You just remember that, Captain." She could hear the warmth of humor in his own voice. "Seriously, they would be comforted if I joined them in a ritual that would continue through the entire length of the journey."

"I don't like the idea of you being away from *Voyager* at such a critical time," Janeway said.

"Neither do I, but I like even less the idea of the Lamorians staying behind."

So did his captain. She thought about it, then sighed. "Very well."

"I'll be returning for some supplies and my medicine bundle."

"We'll talk then. Janeway out." No sooner had she finished than Kim said, "It's the Todanians. Leader Arkathi has some suggestions for you."

I'll bet he does, Janeway thought. She closed her eyes, gathering strength.

Finally, after fifteen and a half hours of Janeway coaxing, cajoling, ordering, bullying, compromising, and otherwise doing everything she could, the remaining thirty ships in the caravan agreed to go through the nebula.

Voyager would do so without some of her crew. Chakotay, of course, would be conducting a religious ceremony aboard the Lamorian ship. Two other ships had expressed such terror at negotiating blindly through the nebula that Janeway had sent her second- and third-shift conn officers to their vessels. Interestingly enough, the Kuluuk, who might have been expected to request aid, and who indeed had been offered it, had refused. They seemed embarrassed by the incident in engineering, and wanted to navigate the nebula on their own.

Paris, of course, was going nowhere. She needed his expertise. Torres had sent Vorik and Carey to two more ships, figuring that their engineering expertise would help them handle any problems that might come up. Janeway realized that while *Voyager* would probably come through this nebula with no trouble, some of these other ships on which her crew would be temporarily serving might not fare as well. But it was the best way to ensure that everyone made it through safely.

Finally, the time arrived. She settled down in her command chair, purposefully ignoring the empty chair to her left. For a moment, she treated herself to the luxury of simply admiring the nebula's beauty: swirls of soft blue and purple, twining mists of color, enlivened by the occasional flash. Deceptively attractive.

"Engage," she said. "One-half impulse."

"Aye, Captain," Paris said, with more than his usual formality.

Slowly, the ship glided forward. For a moment, nothing happened, and they could see on the screen the lovely colors closing softly about their ship.

The lights began to flash erratically, then went out. Janeway didn't have to order the emergency lights. The bloodred lights came on automatically, bathing everyone and everything in an eerie crimson glow. "Status."

"Tactical is down," said Tuvok.

"Intership operations sporadic, but continuing for the moment," said Kim. "Shields are down. Sensors are inoperative."

"Helm responding," said Paris.

"Astrometrics will not be of use, Captain," came Seven's voice.

134

The image of swirling blue and purple on the screen flickered. They would lose visual soon.

"Tuvok, launch the first buoy," Janeway ordered.

"Launching." They all watched in silence as the small, circular probe hurtled out, spun, then stopped. "Engineering, engage frequency."

Janeway didn't quite hold her breath, but she breathed shallowly. This would be the determining factor. If she was wrong, if there was no frequency that could be heard through the swirls of ion gases, then the idea would not be feasible. They'd have to either find some other way to get all these ships safely through, or else abandon the plan and take the lengthy, dangerous trip around the nebula.

And there it was. A soft hum, barely audible, but there. "Paris, back us away. Slowly."

He did so. The crisp, clear image on the screen grew fuzzy and was broken up by black and white, screeching static. Finally, they could see nothing but static on the screen. The sound increased, but through it all, Janeway could still hear the reassuring hum of the probe.

"Distance?" she asked.

"Twenty kilometers," Kim counted. "A hundred. Two hundred. Five hundred."

"It's still audible, even to the naked human ear," said Paris.

"One thousand," Kim continued. "Two thousand." Now it was becoming increasingly hard to hear the frequency of the probe. "Three thousand."

"And there it goes," said Paris. "We've lost the signal lock."

"I can't hear it anymore, either," said Janeway. The sound was lost in the static.

"I can," said Tuvok. Janeway glanced over at him, suppressing a smile. She'd not make so obvious a joke at his expense.

"Let's opt for fifteen hundred," said Janeway. "Not all ears may be as sharp as Commander Tuvok's." *Nor will all the technology be up to* Voyager*'s level,* she thought. "All right, Tom. Let's keep going."

CHAPTER

11

CHAKOTAY WAITED ON THE BRIDGE WITH OPHAR, daughter of Willar, son of Tymu, and her crew. The only reason there was a floor and walls was because a ship of necessity had to have such things. Various consoles were located literally everywhere, on the floor, as on *Voyager*, on the walls, on the ceiling. The Lamorians had very kindly adjusted their gravity to accommodate him, though, had the positive outcome of the situation depended on it, Chakotay would have been willing to wait the entire time in zero g.

The Lamorians were small, hovering spheres with retractable tentacles. They were also excruciatingly polite and filled with a love and respect for ritual that bordered on the obsessive. They were the ones who had almost lost a crewman—crewthing?—to Neelix's chocolate soufflé. Chakotay found himself

137

growing quite fond of them. Though they were extremely rigid among themselves about their rituals, they understood that not every species behaved the same way and were quite tolerant of the dozen or so faux pas he'd managed to make already.

They were the twenty-first ship to go through. Janeway had kept the ships that were playing host to her crewmen far down on the list, so that they could offer their advice to as many as possible before the ships to which they were temporarily assigned passed through the nebula.

The viewscreen took up almost all the space on the floor (of course, to the Lamorians, "floor" was a variable concept). Chakotay found it a bit disturbing to be walking on a window, but he now sat down and watched with the others as ship after ship lined up.

First to go through after *Voyager* would be the Nenlar ship. It would be a good test. It was a smaller vessel, and not nearly as well equipped to navigate the nebula as *Voyager.* The Nenlars would be close enough to *Voyager* to call for help should they find any problems. He watched as the little ship disappeared into the swirling mists of blue and purple.

Next were the Iyal, then the Tllihuh, then . . . which one was that? It was getting so hard to keep track of all these different ships. He marveled that Janeway did it so easily. Though she had played down her accomplishments, Chakotay knew that she was performing as well as any formal ambassador could have.

Suddenly Chakotay frowned. Four—no, five—no, eight—ships were breaking rank. They moved upward, jumping their place in line.

"May I use your communications systems?" asked Chakotay.

Ophar flicked a tentacle and a red light went on in the ceiling. "This is Commander Chakotay, first officer of *Voyager.* I'm presently assigned to the Lamorian vessel. What's going on? Return to your positions in the line at once."

A crackle, and then the ominous visage of the Hirogen Alpha appeared, filling the entire floor of the Lamorian ship.

"Commander Chakotay," he said, scornfully. "This is ridiculous. Our ship is practically the last one to venture through."

"That was so you could assist any vessel that you found in trouble. You said you'd be willing to help."

The Alpha waved a hand in a gesture of impatience. "Several ships have already gone through. We are tired of waiting—tired of constantly taking a backseat to prey." Abruptly the conversation was terminated as the *Rhev* zipped past six other ships and disappeared into the nebula.

Chakotay recognized the Iudka vessel and swore under his breath. The assembled Lamorians emitted a high-pitched whistle of offense, but he couldn't take the time to soothe their riled emotions now.

"Chakotay to *Nivvika.* Cease your advance." Even as he spoke, he saw the *Relka* dip and dive past the waiting ships. Trust Sinimar Arkathi to buck the rules. The Iudka ship did not answer, and a second later it was gone.

"Make them stop!" bleated Ophar. "They are not following the rules! They are creating disorder!"

"You're telling me," muttered Chakotay. "Please,

everyone, this nebula is dangerous. You need to go one at a time and follow the buoys. There is a chance that without this order someone will get lost or there will be a collision, or . . ."

He let his voice trail off. It was hopeless. There were now a couple of dozen ships that had abandoned their places in line and were rushing forward, crowding one another in their haste to leap into the nebula. He supposed he should count himself lucky that no one had opened fire on his neighbor. There was no way to let *Voyager* know of the chaos; the ion gases that interfered with communication while in the nebula made that impossible while they were separated by its swirls. Finally, after about fifteen minutes, things settled down. Those who had wanted to forge ahead and ignore the order that Janeway had spent hours hashing out with everyone involved had done so and were gone. The ships that remained behind, only a handful or so, closed up the gaps in their lines and waited for his command.

"Chakotay to Kuluuk vessel *Eru*."

The face of Tarna, leader of the Kuluuk, filled the viewscreen. "Responding, Commander." Tarna's paws were fluttering about, now touching its round face, now patting the arms of the chair. Its face was changing from its normal cherry-red hue to green. A bad sign.

"You've distributed the tranquilizer our doctor manufactured for you?" Chakotay asked.

"Yes," replied Tarna. "But all those ships rushing past—terrifying!"

"They weren't going to hurt you," Chakotay

soothed. "They were just impatient to get going. They were more rude than hostile."

The Kuluuk leader blinked solemnly. "Rudeness *is* hostility."

Chakotay laughed. "Can't argue that one. Still, you're up next. Are you ready to go?"

Tarna took a deep, shuddering breath. The green started to fade. "I think so."

"Take as long as you like. Follow the buoys."

Suddenly the leader's face turned green. "What if Captain Janeway forgot to set the buoys?"

"Impossible."

"What if we can't find them? If we get lost? If the power drain happens again? If we—"

"You'll be fine. There will be ships ahead of you and ships behind you. They will all be willing to help you if you run into any trouble. And if for some reason you do get lost, I promise *Voyager* will return to you."

They reminded him of teddy bears, though there was not much physical resemblance. It was the large eyes and the trusting expression combined with fear, Chakotay supposed. Finally Tarna nodded.

"We will go through now," it said in a voice that quavered.

"You are very brave," said Chakotay, and he meant it.

The enormous visage of the Kuluuk commander disappeared. Chakotay watched with satisfaction as the *Eru* slowly edged toward the nebula, paused for a moment, then went inside.

One more ship moved forward, entered the nebula. "We're next," said Chakotay. Ophar chirped a command and the ship made its way to the edge of the nebula.

"I alone will pilot the vessel," said Ophar. "Chakotay, son of Kolopak, it is time for you to begin. The rest of my crew will join you."

Chakotay nodded. Ophar floated upward. Eight tentacles emerged from her round body and reached to manipulate the controls. She would be fine by herself. Following the buoys would be child's play for this vessel. Chakotay was more concerned about smaller, less technologically advanced ships. They were the ones more likely to miss the buoys, or get caught up in the eddies of the nebula. Still, there was a duty he had to perform, and despite the gnawing doubts at the back of his mind, he was looking forward to it.

Five minutes later, he was seated in a huge, domed room. It was entirely composed of clear material, so he felt as though he were floating in space. It was a bit unsettling. He hurried to sit, to feel the solidness of matter beneath his buttocks and thighs.

There were hundreds of them, some up near what passed for the ceiling, some clinging to the "walls," others nestled right beside him. Obeying the impulse, and knowing he would be immediately forgiven if he transgressed, Chakotay reached to touch one of them. Its skin was smooth and cool, like that of the dolphins he had touched back on Earth. It did not shy away. Rather it snuggled closer to him and made a soft, sweet, cooing noise. Who would have thought it? With all their precise decorum, touching, perhaps the most intimate of contacts, was not only accepted, but welcomed.

Carefully, Chakotay spread out his medicine bundle. It had been a long time since he had last done so. He picked up each item and identified it for the intently listening Lamorians.

"A blackbird's wing," he said. "A stone from the river. The *akoonah,* a way to enter an altered state safely, without dangerous drugs. Although today, we do not wish to enter that state, but to be aware, alert, ready to honor the gods of the Lamorians."

He had perfect timing. At that precise moment, the soft swirls of blue and purple closed in around them. The Lamorians made soft, sighing noises, and, as one, all retracted their tentacles and became simply hovering orbs.

"We are in the presence of the gods," breathed the orb Chakotay had been stroking. "We are surrounded by the divine."

"Let us ask for their blessings in guiding us safely through their realm," said Chakotay, with the utmost solemnity, and began.

We should wait until they are all gone, thought One Who Is Second. *The chance of them detecting us is strong if we enter alongside them.*

One Who Masters Technology gave the mental equivalent of a snort of derision. *Their sensors will be rendered useless,* it sent. *You heard the One Who Is Janeway. There is only a limited visual range for the other vessels. We could pass right by them and not be detected. We could do that now, if we wanted to.*

But there is no point in tempting fate, cautioned One Who Braves Strangers. Even it, experienced as it was with interacting with other species, did not like to invite such contact. And if they were detected, all would be lost.

One Who Is Leader sat and "listened" quietly. It would reserve judgment until all thoughts were aired. Privately, it had its own opinion, but among his people, a good Leader was one who did what the majority wanted as often as it could.

And if, Masters Technology, Second continued, *their sensors are so impaired by the ion gases of this nebula, what will happen to ours? Who is to say that once we enter that nebula, we will not become suddenly visible to them?*

Masters Technology's thoughts were almost fragrant with scorn. *It won't happen. The ion gas does not affect things in that manner. The worst that could happen would be that we, too, would have to be navigating blindly. And if that is so, then—*

Then we could collide with another ship! Leader winced at the intensity of Second's thoughts. *We could become forever lost!*

What would you have us do? Masters Technology shot back. *If we wait until they are all through, the buoys might be gone. Our chances of getting lost would significantly increase. And what if the caravan has gone by the time we make it through? We might not be able to pick up their trail again. And then we would be on our own. Is that your desire, Second?*

Enough, sent Leader calmly. *I have received all input, acknowledged all views. I believe Masters Technology is correct. We should shadow a ship on the caravan.*

With respect, Leader, thought Second, although there was little respect in the flavor of his thoughts, *you have seen the chaos that occurred earlier, when they all crowded one another in their primitive eagerness to cross the nebula. I might have agreed had they all not deviated from One Who Is Janeway's instructions, but now, their actions are unpredictable. They are dangerous.*

Second, I have made my decision. We will proceed. Masters Technology, shadow a ship that has displayed calmness in this confusion. Pick a large, technologically advanced vessel.

A ship with advanced technology is more likely to detect us, cautioned Braves Strangers.

True, acknowledged Leader. *But it is also less likely to become lost, and its size will enable us to track it more easily.*

Masters Technology pulled up several ships on the viewscreen. *One Who Is Janeway assigned her One Who Is Second to this vessel here,* it sent, indicating a large ship. *It is just about to enter the nebula. It fits your criteria, Leader, plus it has one of the humans on it.*

An excellent choice, approved Leader. *Let us become its shadow.*

Slowly, carefully, leaving as much space as possible between their vessel and those of the strangers, they maneuvered into position slightly above and behind the designated vessel.

It took *Voyager* four hours, sometimes dropping to quarter impulse, to negotiate their way through the nebula. It was trickier than they had expected, and more than once they got mired in an unexpected eddy.

"Just call me Hansel," said Paris, as they dropped the twelfth buoy.

"Let's hope our bread crumbs stay in place," said Janeway, feigning a humor she did not feel. She knew they would get through all right. But what about the little ships? The short-range vessels, the ones with less advanced technology? That was where cooperation between the vessels that composed this cobbled-together fleet was of the utmost importance. If they all looked out for one another, then they all would get through.

Then she thought of the anger of Sinimar Arkathi, of the terror the Nenlar had for the Iudka, of the faces of the now-dead Ammunii, and despair knifed through her.

Dear God, who am I kidding? she thought. *If we get through this without a war in miniature, we'll be lucky.*

Another two hours and fourteen buoys later, and the ion bombardment began to decrease.

"We're coming out of it," said Kim.

"About time," said Paris.

"We have left a total of twenty-six buoys," Tuvok said. "That should leave an easily navigable trail."

"Let's hope you're right," said Janeway. "Now all we do is sit and wait. The Nenlars should be appearing at any moment."

But they didn't.

Voyager waited. And waited.

CHAPTER

12

THE NENLARS HAD BEEN RIGHT BEHIND THEM. THEY
had been close enough to have signaled for aid if
they were on the verge of getting lost in the nebula
swirls. Yet *Voyager* had heard nothing.

When the two-man vessel finally emerged, seem-
ing even tinier than Janeway had remembered it, she
let out a sigh of relief.

"*Voyager* to Torar and Ara. You two gave us a bit
of a scare."

"We had some scares ourselves, Captain," came
Torar's voice. It was laden with tension. "We lost
you shortly after the third buoy."

Janeway nodded to herself. That had been one of
the trickier ones to negotiate. "But you found the
path back," she said reassuringly. "Well done. Let's
hope those who followed you did as good a job."

About twenty minutes later, the Iyal came through. They had not had the problems the Nenlars had had; in fact, they had had no problems at all. Janeway wasn't surprised. The Iyal vessel was comparable to *Voyager.*

One by one, at approximately half-hour intervals, ships emerged. Janeway was just beginning to permit herself to think they'd make it through this with no problems when the next half-hour interval turned into an hour. Then an hour and a half. Then two hours.

Paris turned to face his captain from his seat at the conn. "With your permission, Captain," he said, "Ensign Kim and I could take the *Delta Flyer* and begin searching for the lost ships."

Her eyes on the screen, Janeway shook her head. "Not yet, Mr. Paris. Let's give them a little more time." *If only there were some way to communicate with Chakotay, on the other side of the nebula,* she thought. He'd be able to tell her if there was anything to worry about. It could simply be that the next ship in line was having trouble. That inexplicable energy drain could have struck yet another vessel, and since Janeway had insisted that they proceed in strict order, one ship with problems could delay the whole process.

She had almost convinced herself that that was the case when all of a sudden several ships seemed to explode from the nebula all at once. Heading the pack was the Hirogen ship, but hard on their heels were the Iudka and the Todanian ships. More came out, flying so closely they almost touched. Janeway spotted fresh damage on more than one vessel and cursed softly. As she had feared, not going in order had led more than a few vessels to collide in the density of the nebula.

Before, she had hailed each ship, and received a calm answer in reply. Now, several ships tried to hail her at once.

"Captain Janeway! The Yumiri ship deliberately crashed into our—"

"Captain, I insist you reprimand the Hirogen. They—"

"We tried to follow the buoys, but they were—"

By now, poor Kim was used to this, and managed to isolate the messages. First was the Salamar. Janeway was surprised at such agitation from Ellia, normally so balanced and rational. When Kim got her image onscreen, her ears were completely flat against her sleek head.

"It was deliberate!" Ellia repeated. "We insist that we be compensated for the damage to our ship. Surely you can see it!"

Janeway could. While she spoke, she signaled to Kim to get the Yumiri captain. "I do see it, Commander, but I'm certain it was an accident. With that many ships going through all at once"—and even as she spoke, about fifteen more ships emerged—"this was bound to happen. I've got the Yumiri captain and I'll patch him through to you. Janeway out." She jerked her head in Harry's direction. "Next, Mr. Kim."

"The buoys were scattered." It was the deep voice of the Hirogen Alpha. As he materialized on the screen, Janeway could see the contempt on his ugly face. "There were several places where there were no buoys at all and we had to use our own best judgment. Fortunately," and his voice dripped scorn, "it was sufficient. Your plan is in shambles, Captain Janeway."

Janeway narrowed her blue eyes, but didn't bother to rise. She wouldn't give him the satisfaction. "I have a hunch that your vessel was one of the first to break formation, Alpha. And by doing so, you jeopardized the entire process. Of course the buoys got scattered. Some three dozen ships coming through all at once? No one could have expected anything else. I've already seen damage to several vessels. Fortunately, so far, it looks like everyone's managed to limp out on their own after you and those who emulated you ruined the plan. Janeway out."

"Captain," said Tuvok, "we are not at all certain that the Hirogen were the first to break formation."

"Call it a gut feeling, Tuvok, but I'm betting that Chakotay will confirm it. If they weren't the first, I am at least dead certain they were right behind the first. It's not in the Hirogen nature to take commands from prey, especially if they disagree."

"Captain," said Kim, "I've got Arkathi waiting. He claims that the Iudka harassed them in the nebula, even tried to board."

"Let Arkathi wait until everyone else is accounted for," said Janeway. Time enough to deal with her major annoyance when she knew for certain they wouldn't have to perform any rescue missions.

She felt a surge of relief when all the vessels with her crew aboard came through all right, and an extra jolt of pleasure when she saw the Lamorian ship.

"Chakotay to Janeway," came the familiar voice. "I see you have already guessed that several ships failed to follow instructions." His face appeared on the viewscreen. Several dozen of the spherical Lamorians hovered around him.

"Indeed," said Janeway dryly. "We're lucky that we haven't lost anyone so far." She stepped down toward the viewscreen. "Settle a bet between me and Tuvok," she continued, fighting a smile. "Was it the Hirogen who got fed up with waiting first?"

"You win, Captain. It certainly was. But Arkathi and the Iudka weren't far behind." He frowned. "We're still missing a few, aren't we?"

Janeway nodded. "The aforementioned Iudka and the Kuluuk, among others. By the way, how did our little green friends fare?"

"For them, with great courage," Chakotay said with respect. "I think if they ever do return home, they're going to bring a new spirit of adventure and bravery to their people."

"Let's hope their emperor can see the value in that," said Janeway.

As she spoke, the Iudka vessel cleared the nebula. At once, Kelmar's voice came through loud and clear at Kim's station.

"Captain Janeway, I wish to formally report an attack by the Nenlar upon our vessel."

"Kelmar, you're not the first to assume that an accidental brushing in the thick of that nebula constituted an attack," said Janeway. "We've already had several—"

"I know what we saw, Captain! I demand that you hold an inquiry into this immediately!"

"You'll have to take your place in line," said Janeway wearily. All this sniping, argument, uncooperation. Why was it necessary? The Nenlar and the Iudka aside, most of these races didn't even know one another. Why was everyone so quick to assume the worst?

"Captain, I—"

"Your complaint will be heard, Kelmar, but not until everyone is present and accounted for. We're still waiting for a few stragglers. That tops my list. Janeway out."

"I'm beginning to hope that we will have to take the *Flyer* into the nebula in search of stragglers," said Paris. "It would be better than trying to wade through all this finger-pointing."

"I'll always prefer verbal violence over actual violence, Mr. Paris," said Janeway, "but your point is well taken. Actively doing good beats listening to squabbling any day."

Hours passed. Six more ships straggled out, but there was no sign of the Kuluuk. Finally, Janeway sighed. She turned to Chakotay, who had beamed aboard from the Lamorian vessel.

"You saw them last," she said. "What do you think?"

"They were frightened, of course," Chakotay replied, "but I didn't think there'd be all that much in there to really alarm them. They were prepared for perhaps drifting off course, or missing the buoys, and I told them help would be available from anyone in the caravan. They had administered the tranquilizer the Doctor had given them. I think if they haven't found their way out by now they may be in real trouble. Tarna did mention that his was one of the vessels that had been having a problem with power drains."

"Agreed. Mr. Paris, you and Mr. Kim are up. Take the *Flyer* and retrace the route." She knew that there was a very real chance that the small vessel might get lost, but Kim and Paris were two of the best. The Kuluuk needed to be rescued, and the *Flyer,* manned by these two, was their best hope.

"Yes, ma'am," said Paris. He and Kim headed quickly for the turbolift.

Godspeed, Janeway thought, but did not say.

For all his jaunty attitude, Paris wasn't overly keen about venturing back into the nebula. It was a very real risk they were taking, and though he was confident in his and Kim's skills, he was still a little nervous as the swirling haze of blue and purple closed in about them.

"It's probably nothing," said Kim. "Knowing the Iudka, they got scared and passed out."

"I wish there had been some other way to get them through this."

"You heard Commander Chakotay. He said they were feeling up to the challenge."

For a long time, they flew slowly through the colorful whorls. They passed the first three probes, which were in their appointed places.

"Where's the fourth?" Kim asked.

"Gone," said Paris. And so was the fifth, and the sixth, and the seventh. The eighth was still there, but wildly off course. Paris swore under his breath. "No wonder people were so edgy when they finally made it through. This looks like we were incredibly sloppy."

"We weren't," protested Kim.

"Of course we weren't. We know that. But if you

were a ship following us, what would you be thinking along about now?"

Kim opened his mouth to reply, paused, then said, smiling a little, "That we were incredibly sloppy."

At that moment, the static on the viewscreen cleared suddenly. Paris had to veer hard to port to avoid flying directly into the Kuluuk ship.

There it was, hanging at an awkward angle, dead in space. Paris swore softly. Well, at least it wasn't an enormous vessel. At best, the *Flyer*'s tractor beam could manage it alone. If the tractor beam didn't have to extend for a long distance, it should work all right. At worst, he could find them again, leading *Voyager* straight to the ship.

Paris brought the vessel close to the *Eru*'s bridge. The closer they could get to the communications systems, the more likely they'd be to hear any distress calls.

"*Delta Flyer* to the *Eru*. Come in, *Eru*."

Static screeched, then silence. Tom frowned. He was flying right above the ship. Even in the nebula, with this kind of proximity to the bridge, he ought to be hearing something.

He tried again, but was again met only with static, then silence.

"This isn't good," said Harry.

"Can you clean up the channel?"

"That's what I'm trying to do," Harry replied, his fingers flying over the controls. He shook his dark head. "Sorry. It's as clear as we're going to get it, Tom. They simply aren't responding."

"The captain was afraid of this," said Paris. "Those Kuluuk. Navigating this thing probably scared them senseless. I bet they're cowering in a corner somewhere and—"

He froze in midsentence. B'Elanna's words in the mess hall floated back to him: *Apparently the Kuluuk are extremely timid. A good scare can literally kill them.*

"Oh, no," he breathed. "Harry, can we scan for life-forms?"

"Only within a twenty-meter radius. You think something's happened?"

"I hope not." He waited impatiently while Kim tried to reconfigure the sensors. Finally, Kim shook his dark head.

"No luck."

Paris swore. "Any way we can transport to that ship?"

"Not while we're in the nebula," said Kim. "Why?"

"We've got to board it. I think there's something wrong. You've heard the phrase 'scared to death'? Well, with the Kuluuk, that's a very real possibility."

"You're kidding." Tom looked at him. "You're not kidding. I knew they were timid, but—okay." He leaned back in his chair, thinking. A second later, he bolted upright. "The pattern enhancers. If we can attach ourselves to the ship, we might be able to transport the enhancers one at a time into it. We can activate them from here and it might be enough to transport one of us safely."

"That'd be me," said Paris, already rising and getting out three of the tripod enhancers. Thank goodness they were standard equipment on every shuttle.

"Tom, if there's any danger, I'm more expendable than *Voyager*'s best pilot. Especially now, with this convoy to lead."

"Don't even try it, Harry. You're much better at this transport reconfiguration mumbo jumbo than I am, and besides, I'm heading this mission, remember?"

Kim didn't start working on the transporter immediately. "It's very risky."

"Then you'd better make sure I come home in one piece. I'd hate to think of what B'Elanna would do to you if you lost me." He winked. Reluctantly, Harry turned back to the transporter.

"Okay, let's give it a whirl," said Kim. He touched a padd and the familiar hum of the transporter filled the shuttle. The first pattern enhancer shimmered and began to fade out. It reappeared, faded, reappeared, and finally faded for a final time. Kim repeated the transport twice more, honing the frequency each time.

"Well," said Tom, "that was not the most reassuring thing I've ever seen. How are they doing?"

"They've materialized aboard the Kuluuk ship. They appear to be stable. Cross your fingers while I activate them." Paris waited, tense, then Kim said, "They're on." He turned to look at Paris. "We've got a transporter energy spike. You're good to go." He hesitated, then said, "Good luck, Tom."

"You watch that thing and make sure I don't end up as scattered molecules, all right?" Paris said with a humor he didn't feel.

Kim managed a wan smile. "Can't lose Captain Proton."

"Damn right. Okay, let's do it."

* * *

Paris materialized in a large, brightly lit room decorated with colorful furnishings. He guessed it was some kind of meeting room, though it was empty at the moment. He glanced at the little red chairs and blue tables, and felt for a moment like Gulliver among the Lilliputians, or a guest at one of the tea parties Naomi Wildman used to host when she was younger.

"Paris to Kim. Can you hear me?"

"You're breaking . . . static . . . can hear you." Kim's voice was barely audible amid the screech of static, but it was there.

"Okay, you're breaking up too. I'll be back here in a half hour if not sooner. Paris out."

He took a deep breath and stepped into the corridor. "Hello," he called, hoping that the translator on his combadge was working. "This is Ensign Paris from *Voyager*. We found your ship. Are you all right?"

Silence was the only answer. Paris swallowed hard. He had a very bad feeling about this. He tried to activate his tricorder, but the readings were erratic. Just in case the lights went out on him without warning, he turned on his wristlight.

"Hello to the Kuluuk. This is Tom Paris from *Voyager*. Can anybody hear me?"

No one answered. Grimly, he pressed on, walking alone through the small corridors, having to duck his head to enter room after room.

It was on the bridge where he found the bodies.

They lay dead at their posts, their small, furry forms sprawled as if they had suddenly fallen asleep and tumbled from their colorful chairs. Paris's throat constricted.

"Ah, damn it to hell," he muttered, sorrow welling inside him. Just to make sure, he went from body to body, gently feeling for a pulse with the utmost respect. They were cold and stiffening. He didn't know enough about their physiology to hazard a guess as to when they had died. It didn't matter. It was obvious with this species what had happened.

A good scare can literally kill them.

What had been that fatal fright? Entering the nebula in the first place? Or had they summoned up the courage to do that, trusting enough to follow *Voyager*'s lead? Had their multiple hearts failed them when they drifted out of range of the buoys? Or had a ship passed dangerously close? They would never know for certain.

Sighing, Paris rose. There was no need to check further for survivors. Surely the crew staffing the bridge would be the most courageous Kuluuk on the ship. If they succumbed to terror, Paris knew in his heart that the rest of the crew had died of fright as well.

He was turning to leave when something caught his eye. He wasn't sure what, and turned his head to look again. Something was out of the ordinary. *Well, yeah, everyone's dead,* his conscious mind told his more perceptive inner mind. But that wasn't it.

Slowly, Paris walked around the bridge again, looking at but not touching the small corpses. He paused when he came to the captain, and stared at him anew.

That was it.

Tarna wasn't slumped naturally in his chair, or even in a huddled ball at the foot of it. He was rigid and his head was at an odd angle. Kneeling in front of the body, Paris looked closer to confirm his suspicion. His neck had been broken, and obviously not by a fall.

Someone had murdered the Kuluuk captain.

Immediately Paris rose and drew his phaser. That someone could still be on board the ship, hiding, awaiting his chance, certain that he could remain undetected thanks to the ions disrupting the sensors.

It was possible, but not likely. Paris made his way quickly back to the transport site, senses keenly alert for any sound. More likely, he thought as he hastened down the corridors, the killer had come as an ally and then brutally murdered Tarna. Even for staunch Kuluuk, the sight of such treachery probably would have been enough to kill them. The killer then could rampage through the ship, on a coward's mission. Simply screaming at the Kuluuk, already afraid about going into the nebula at all, would probably have been enough. Brandishing a weapon, or killing the captain on his own bridge—well, Kuluuk genetics would accomplish results a mass murderer would be proud of. And the bastard wouldn't have had to touch more than a single person to do it.

Anger was growing inside him. Paris began to wish the killer would make an appearance. He'd never heard of anything so lily-livered in his whole life. What kind of monster would do such a thing? And for God's sake, *why?*

One thought alone comforted him as he transported back to the *Delta Flyer,* and that was what

Captain Janeway was going to do with the murderer once she got her hands on him.

He only hoped he'd get to watch.

As Paris had expected, Janeway reacted with an emotion that made "furious" look like "mildly annoyed."

When they had emerged from the nebula, knowing that anyone would be able to hear him, he had sent a message saying only that the Kuluuk ship would be unable to get out under its own power and would need a tow. Once aboard ship, Paris and Kim had spoken with their captain in private. Now Paris felt a keen sense of pleasure at watching her eyes flash with righteous rage and the color rise in her cheeks. He wanted badly to hear a loud, angry rant, but when she spoke her voice was cold and her words precise.

"Did you find anything to indicate who might have done it?"

"Only that it had to be someone that the Kuluuk trusted, and that they were strong enough to break the captain's neck," Paris answered. "It was obviously not an accident."

"Almost any species in the caravan could do that," said Kim.

"And we've been doing our damnedest to promote trust among the various species," said Janeway. "We encouraged communication. To think of those gentle little beings, thinking that someone was coming to help them. . . ." With a visible effort, she forced her emotions down. "Tell no one what happened until we know for certain. No one, do you understand?"

They nodded.

"Dismissed. Send in Commanders Tuvok and Chakotay. And gentlemen—"

She now smiled calmly, and there was no more hint of outrage on her attractive features. "Don't give this game away. I want you to wear your best poker faces."

"Yes, ma'am," said Paris. But even as he left, he wondered how good his best poker face was going to be when it was called upon to hide pain, outrage, and a sickening sense of injustice.

CHAPTER 13

SILENCE LAY HEAVILY UPON THE ONES WHO WILL NOT Be Named. It was not the silence of unspoken words, for that was never experienced on their ships. It was the silence of unformed thoughts. No one had any idea what to do with the dreadful knowledge they harbored.

What do we do? asked Masters Technology at length.

Leader did not answer right away. It stared out the enormous viewscreen and watched as the ship called *Voyager* appeared out of the nebula. It towed the dead ship.

We need to tell them, thought Braves Strangers. Its thoughts were laced with the certainty of the righteous.

That's fine for someone who is familiar with Strangers to say, replied Second, harshly. *And if we were not in such a perilous position ourselves, I might be inclined to agree with you. But here, now? How are we to know that they would believe us? We have been following them, keeping ourselves hidden. From what I understand about most species, that would make them inclined to suspect us, not to trust us. We cannot risk revealing ourselves for Strangers!*

They were the most innocent of all Strangers I have ever encountered, Braves Strangers fired back. Its thoughts were almost painful to receive, so laden with emotion were they. *Gentle beings with no hatred toward others. So gentle they could not handle being in a place where they were not loved and protected.*

Too fragile, thought Second. *They could not endure. If they had not been killed, they would have died anyway at some point.*

That is not the point, said Leader, its thoughts hard and certain. *The point is, they offered harm toward none. They trusted, and for that trust, they were brutally slain. We saw. We watched it happen, and did not intervene. We bear a certain amount of guilt for that as much as the killers do. I—I now regret that decision.*

What? Second was shocked. *Leader, you did absolutely the right thing in not interfering with the natural course of conflict between these species. We have nothing to do with that. We should have nothing to do with that.*

It was wrong, and it is wrong now to keep our silence. Yet for the safety of you, my crew, I shall continue to do so. Masters Technology, can you tell us anything more about the power drain?

Masters Technology thought unhappy thoughts. Finally it sent, *I am as ignorant as the* Voyager *engineer, or any of the others. But one thing I feel cer-*

tain of, and that is that it is caused by the gateway. Whether it occurred the moment we went through, or is being caused by the other gateways, that much I believe.

Leader turned again to regard the mass of ships, all halted, all waiting for orders. One of those ships housed only corpses and those investigating the crime. Another vessel housed the killers of the Kuluuk. The Ones Who Will Not Be Named knew everything about every ship. They knew who could be trusted, who could not, who planned treachery, and who was the next target. Leader ached inside with the guilt it carried. It was not an unfamiliar sensation, but associating it with aliens was new indeed. Could it be that they really were as worthy, in their own strange and unfathomable fashions, as the Ones Who Will Not Be Named? Could it be that each one of their lives mattered as much to their kin and colleagues as those of Leader's crew did to it?

It had not shielded its thoughts. It sensed Masters Technology's worry, Second's indignation, Braves Strangers's approval.

This One Who Is Janeway is wise, Leader sent at last. *It is entirely possible that she will determine who the killer is on her own, without aid from us. For the moment, we will wait. And watch.*

And try to solve the problem of our drained energy, added Masters Technology.

"Report," said Janeway. No one had transported to the Kuluuk vessel, and no one would until they had safely towed it into open space. It had been tricky enough once, with Paris making his grim discovery.

She wouldn't risk it again. And in the meantime, she would listen to discover what, if anything, Torres had learned about the mysterious power drain that was beginning to cripple more and more vessels.

B'Elanna looked exhausted. She rubbed her eyes as she spoke. "I wish I *had* something to report. Everything seems to be functioning within normal parameters."

"On the Salamar ship as well?"

Torres nodded wearily. "I worked side by side with their engineers. Unless there's something they're not telling me, which I think is pretty unlikely, then I can't figure it out. Their ship will power up fine, but within a few hours it's as if it's one of Tom's holographic jalopies—"

"Hey, my cars are not jalopies!" interjected Paris.

"—and it's just run out of gas," Torres continued as if Paris hadn't spoken. By way of apology, she placed her hand on his for a brief moment and squeezed. "It's the strangest thing I've ever seen. Then, once they've been dead for a while, they'll suddenly start up again. But each time, the power resurge lasts for a shorter time. Captain, I'll admit it—I have no clue as to what's going on."

Janeway knew what the admission cost her chief engineer and didn't belabor it. Torres was capable, experienced, intelligent, and imaginative. If she couldn't figure it out, she doubted that anyone else could.

"And the same thing is happening with both ships?"

"It's identical."

Janeway leaned back in her chair, considering. "It has to have something to do with the gateways."

"But how? And why now? And why some ships and not others, and some ships more than others?" Janeway got the impression that Torres could keep coming up with questions all day, if she were allowed to.

"Well," Janeway said with a slight smile, "it certainly gives you something to do while we're all stuck here, doesn't it?"

"Bridge to Janeway," came Kim's voice.

"Go ahead," she replied.

"We've cleared the nebula." A pause. "I've tried hailing the Kuluuk vessel, but there is no response. Their communications systems must have been damaged." He did a good job of keeping his voice neutral, but Janeway and Paris, the only other two who knew what bleakness the vessel housed, stiffened a little. Their eyes met briefly before Paris glanced away.

Janeway didn't like ordering a man to lie to his wife, or a loyal ensign to lie to his senior officers. She debated telling everyone right now, but decided against it. The fewer people who knew, at the moment, the better.

"Thank you, Mr. Kim. Keep trying. If we continue to get no response, we'll transport a team over to assist them in the repairs." God, she hated this. "Torres, keep at it. I want an update as soon as you know anything."

Torres rose. "Aye, Captain."

"Dismissed." She waited until most of them had filed out of the room, then, as if in an afterthought, said, "Oh—Tuvok, Chakotay, Doctor—a moment more of your time?"

Obediently they turned and waited. When the

door hissed closed, Janeway nodded for them to resume their seats.

"We've got a bad situation," she said without preamble. "Everyone aboard the Kuluuk vessel is dead."

A soft sound escaped Chakotay. "I truly believed they could handle it," he said, grief in his voice.

"They could," said Janeway, her gaze flickering between her first officer and her security officer. "Someone saw to it that they didn't make it. Paris reported that the captain's neck had been deliberately broken. There were no other signs of injuries and the broken neck could easily have been overlooked. I'm betting that the killer *counted* on it being overlooked, in fact. Whoever did it wanted us to believe the Kuluuk simply died of fright."

Chakotay swore under his breath. Even Tuvok sat up straighter, his dark eyes narrowing ever so slightly in what passed for Vulcan outrage.

The Doctor had no such compunctions. "That's barbaric!" he exclaimed. "Who would do such a thing to such a gentle people?"

"We don't know—yet. Paris didn't have the chance to conduct a thorough investigation," Janeway continued. "Nor should he have, not alone and with a killer perhaps still on board. This is your job, Tuvok. I want you to go over every inch of that place and find me the killer, or killers, and their motivations. Until you have some answers, I want none of you to say anything. Tuvok, as I said, you'll lead the investigation. I'd like for you to keep it to yourself, but if you need assistance, I know you know who to bring in from your staff. Chakotay, you're the point man on this. I don't want to be seen as being overly concerned, and everyone knows that you had a particular interest in the Kuluuk. Doctor, you of course will be required to perform a few autopsies."

They all nodded somberly. "Dismissed." As they rose to leave, Janeway leaned back in her own chair and took a deep breath. Not a single step on this peculiar journey had been easy, and now, it had turned into a nightmare. She rose and returned to the bridge, fashioning the lies to deflect the interest of the other ships even as she had to order them to stay put, and trying—and failing—not to visualize a ship full of small, furry corpses.

Clad in an enviro-suit that would completely eliminate the possibility that his body might contaminate any evidence he might discover, Tuvok materialized directly on the bridge of the Kuluuk vessel. He was not shocked at the sight; he had known to expect it. Nor was he grieved, or appalled. Such emotions would be unseemly for a Vulcan and for a security chief alike. But he did experience a moment of regret for the senseless loss of life, and a determination to bring the killers to justice.

He touched his combadge and activated his tricorder. "Tuvok to Chakotay." Chakotay had gone to the transporter room so they could communicate privately. "I am presently on the bridge. My tricorder is detecting no signs of life. Mr. Paris did not exaggerate the scope of the incident."

"I'm glad it's you there and not me," came Chakotay's voice.

Tuvok stepped over to the captain and scanned in the visual image of the corpse, making certain the tricorder recorded the image of the head hanging at such an unnatural angle. "Captain Tarna's neck does appear as to have been intentionally broken."

"I'm locking on to him," said Chakotay. "He'll go directly to sickbay. The Doctor's waiting."

Tuvok watched impassively as the body dematerialized. "I will now begin an extensive sweep of the entire vessel. From time to time, I will contact you. Tell the Doctor to expect more bodies. We will need to autopsy more than one to confirm exactly what transpired here."

"Acknowledged. I'll retire to my quarters. Chakotay out."

Tuvok had debated bringing along other security personnel, but in the end had decided against it. There would be less of a chance of contaminating the evidence with only a single person, and besides, he knew he could do the job more thoroughly, if not more quickly. He knew his captain was uncomfortable with maintaining the façade and regretted that he could proceed no faster than he was doing. But more than a quick solution, he knew, Janeway wanted the right solution. If she was going to make accusations, they had best be accurate.

It took him a full half hour to sweep just the bridge. The ship was small, but not that small, and he knew he had several hours' worth of work ahead of him. A few things he could surmise already, but as a famous fictional human detective had once said, it was a mistake to theorize without all the data.

With a patience that none but the children of Vulcan could fully appreciate, he went down every corridor, entered every room, and thoroughly analyzed it with his tricorder. Tuvok followed a precise pattern, to minimize his impact on the scene. Hours passed. Once he had completed the task, he contacted Chakotay, had his tricorder transported to *Voyager* so that analysis could begin at once, and had another tricorder transported to him.

With this new tricorder, Tuvok began a fresh investigation: downloading every piece of information the Kuluuk computer contained. This, too, took time, but once the task had been completed, his job here would be done. For the moment.

"Ah, Captain," said the Doctor, smiling as she entered. "I've got something to show you. I've been thinking about our earlier conversation."

"Which one?" asked Janeway wearily. "The one about the mistreated slaves or about the murdered Kuluuk?"

His broad smile faltered. "Neither of those tragic conversations, actually. An earlier, more pleasant one regarding pets and their beneficent effect upon human health. You spoke so eloquently that I decided to give it a try."

Despite the strain of the situation, Janeway found herself smiling. "You're playing with Fluffy? Er, Barkley?"

"Heavens no," said the Doctor. "I have designed a far more suitable holographic pet." With a flourish, he indicated his desk. There, in a small bowl, swam a goldfish.

She felt laughter inside her and tried to quell it. "A *fish?*"

"His name is Bubbles," said the Doctor, proudly.

Janeway couldn't help it. She laughed out loud. The Doctor glared.

"I'm sorry, Doctor," she said, recovering herself. "I do recall hearing that watching fish swim was relaxing. But you can't hold them, or have them curl up at your feet, or stroke them."

"I'm certain Bubbles and I will have a long, positive, healthy master and pet relationship," said the Doctor, somewhat indignantly.

"I'm certain you will," she allowed. "But that's not why you called me down here, is it?"

He softened, saddened. "No, it isn't. Come take a look." She followed him over to where four Kuluuk bodies lay on the beds. "Three of these succumbed to cardiac arrest, triggered by a rush of chemicals aroused by extreme stimulation. In other words, their multiple hearts couldn't handle the level of terror they were experiencing."

In this day and age, of course, the gruesome autopsies of the past, of Y incisions and cracking of rib cages and weighing of organs, were as outdated as a horse and buggy. Computer analysis told them everything they needed to know. So Janeway wasn't looking at shaved, gutted corpses, but at bodies held in stasis. She didn't even have to deal with the smell of decomposition.

But that didn't ease the pain, or the anger.

"The fourth?" she asked, gently prodding the Doctor to continue.

"The fourth, their captain, was, as our observant Mr. Paris guessed, murdered. The neck was broken."

"Any weapons used?"

"None. Whoever did this had the strength to simply seize the head and turn it sharply enough to snap the neck."

Despite herself, Janeway winced, ever so slightly. "Any sign of a struggle?"

"None at all. If it weren't for this one victim, I would be forced to come to the conclusion that the Kuluuk all died of natural causes."

"That confirms what Paris reported. I'll bet Tuvok's investigation will reveal more of the same. Something happened to the *Eru*. Maybe one of those strange power drains. They asked for help, as we told them they should. Someone the Kuluuk trusted boarded the *Eru*, broke Tarna's neck, and killed the others by frightening them to death." She sighed, rubbed her eyes, and shook her head. "Thank you, Doctor. I'll have Chakotay dematerialize the bodies and hold them in a pattern buffer. You may reopen sickbay for business."

As she strode toward the door, she caught sight of Fluffy/Barkley in his designated area. When their eyes met, the little animal wriggled all over. He was intelligent enough to know he could not cross the forcefield the Doctor had erected to keep him confined—she was certain he'd tried once or twice—but skidded right up to it.

She was seized with a longing to pick him up and cuddle him, bury her face in that long, soft fur. But now wasn't the time. As she left, she wondered how the Doctor and Bubbles would fare. Fish might be fun, but there was nothing like touch to convey affection.

In Chakotay's quarters, the first officer and Tuvok silently went over the data that Tuvok had gathered.

There were fibers, flecks of skin, hairs, all kinds of things that could point to an intruder. But when Chakotay brought this up, Tuvok replied flatly, "You will recall Mr. Neelix's plans for an exchange program."

Chakotay stared at him, knowing what was coming. "Don't tell me."

"The Kuluuk had made some remarkable scientific discoveries despite the handicap of their physically fragile systems. Four days ago, representatives from seventeen other ships were invited to visit their vessel. According to Ensign Cray, once the Kuluuk had overcome their terror, they were generous, open hosts."

Chakotay leaned back in his chair and sighed. "Which means, no doubt, that they let seventeen aliens visit all parts of their ship. Including the bridge, where their captain would later be murdered."

"Precisely." Tuvok arched a brow. "When I objected to Neelix's plan, I had no idea that had I been able to halt it, I could have saved myself so much trouble later on."

"So the fact that we have evidence that seventeen non-Kuluuk life-forms were on that bridge—"

"Means very little."

"There's got to be a list of who was there that day for the exchange," said Chakotay. "If, say, no Iudka were ever invited aboard that ship, and we found evidence that an Iudka had been on it, that would clinch it."

"You are an idealist, Commander."

"That glass *could* be half full, Tuvok," Chakotay replied. But as time crawled by, he was beginning to doubt his own words. There seemed to be nothing that—

"Hold on a minute," he said. He was lying on his bed with the tricorder. "How many Kuluuk did the computer say were on that ship?"

"Two hundred and forty-seven," said Tuvok.

For a moment, Chakotay didn't speak. Curious at the other man's silence, Tuvok turned to regard him. "You swept every part of the ship with the tricorder, right?" asked Chakotay, almost rhetorically.

"Of course."

Chakotay looked up from the tricorder and met Tuvok's gaze. "You found only two hundred and forty-six bodies. Someone's gone missing."

CHAPTER 14

CAPTAIN'S LOG, SUPPLEMENTAL. THERE IS NO HELP FOR it. While I would have preferred to wait until Lieutenant Commander Tuvok had definitively identified the murderer—or murderers—I can postpone notifying the other vessels no longer. There is a slim chance that if the missing Kuluuk is a hostage aboard one of the other ships, it may still be alive. Though it might jeopardize the mission, I must take that risk.

But I'm not planning on telling them everything. Not yet, anyway. There's still a chance that our killer might be lulled into a false sense of security and give himself away.

She'd notified her own crew first, of course. Everyone was appalled. Janeway did hear some murmurings of resentment at being kept in the dark for so long, but for the most part, her crew understood.

It was time. She took a deep breath, and began. "To all ships in the caravan, this is Captain Janeway. I regret that I have some tragic news to report. When we went to the aid of the Kuluuk vessel, which had been temporarily lost in the nebula through which we have just traveled, we discovered that all aboard were dead. While this is sad news, it is not as unexpected as it might be with another species. All of you know how timid the Kuluuk were, and how lethal that fear could be to them under traumatic circumstances. However, according to their computer, one crew member is missing. We are wondering if perhaps a visit was extended. If you know the whereabouts of this missing Kuluuk, please notify me at once. We are going to continue to download information from the ship and will decide what to do with the vessel itself later. Janeway out."

She felt Chakotay watching her. He nodded. "Whoever did this wanted us to think that the Kuluuk had died of fright. You want him to continue thinking that we didn't know it was deliberate."

Janeway nodded. "I trust Tuvok to find the answer for us. In the meantime, let's give whoever did this enough rope to hang themselves with." It was one thing to kill an opponent in battle, or in order to protect other lives. She herself had killed under such circumstances and imagined she would probably do so again. She supposed she could even understand killing for personal gain, though she deplored such actions. But massacring the innocent, gentle Kuluuk? That took a monster, or a madman. And the thought that she was traveling with such only lit a fire under her to find and restrain such a creature from doing something like this ever again.

Had he been human, Tuvok would have started to feel sick of the Kuluuk ship. But of course, he was not, so of course, he did not.

But he knew that had he been human, he would.

He had analyzed every centimeter of the *Eru* once before; now he planned to do so again. One thing his working with Chakotay had brought up was the fact that the Kuluuk stores had been seriously depleted. There was no food left, and as the Kuluuk ship had not been designed for long-range missions, it had no replicator technology installed. Other things, too, had been used up. And yet the Kuluuk had never asked for assistance, never indicated that their supplies were even close to running low. Curious.

Another thing he and Chakotay had learned was who had been part of the exchange program. He glanced now at the list: Ensign Cray, from *Voyager.* Lel, an Iudka from the *Nivvika.* Ara, the Nenlar female. The Beta from the Hirogen vessel. Sinimar Arkathi. Ophar, from the Lamorians, as well as many others. It would have made the glass half full, as Chakotay would have put it, if they had been able to download any records during the time that the ship was in the nebula. But of course, no records had been made, as the systems were not functioning.

Tuvok had an additional mission now—to make certain that there were indeed only two hundred and forty-six bodies on the ship. He had made a thorough sweep, hoping to find living beings. Now, he would need to investigate every corner, to find where a dying Kuluuk might have crawled. Despite Captain Janeway's comment to the other ships, he did not think there was a strong likelihood that the killer would have taken a Kuluuk body back to his own ship. It would be the most incriminating evidence imaginable. It was much more likely that he, Tuvok, had simply overlooked a body, much as he disliked having to admit it.

The hours crawled by as Tuvok continued the search. Chakotay checked in from time to time, inquiring how things were progressing. Tuvok thought that the human was growing irritated with the Vulcan's terse replies. But what else was he to do, when there was quite literally nothing to report?

Beside each body, Tuvok set up a stasis field. It was a quintessentially Vulcan thing to do. On a spiritual level, it was right to honor the dead, and on a practical level, the field prevented the bodies from the unpleasant effects of decomposition. Repeatedly, he had to ask Chakotay to beam over more field generators. There were so many dead. Even to a Vulcan, master of his emotions, the loss was to be mourned.

Finally, after several hours, he noticed a brief fluctuation on the tricorder. He frowned, thinking the equipment was malfunctioning. He stepped forward, and all was well. He took a step backward, and the fluctuation, which lasted only a fraction of a second, occurred again.

Tuvok looked down at his feet. He was standing in the corridor. Kneeling, he touched the floor. It seemed to have no openings. He checked the side walls, and they, too, were quite solid.

He looked up and pointed his tricorder at the ceiling. Again, the fluctuation. The Kuluuk were much shorter than humanoids and it was easy for Tuvok to reach up and feel the ceiling. His delicate, questing fingers found what he was looking for: two small buttons. When he pressed them simultaneously, a section of the ceiling slid back.

What he saw caused even the disciplined Vulcan to react with a touch of revulsion.

It was, of course, the missing Kuluuk. It hovered, held in place by a stasis field of unknown origin that kept it in place and also prevented the telltale smell of decomposition from escaping.

There was no way anyone could have imagined that this Kuluuk had died of fright. The corpse was nothing more than a mass of soft tissue. Its entire skeleton had been deftly removed.

There was only one species that Tuvok knew of who routinely kept body parts of other species they had killed.

"Tuvok to Chakotay," he said. "I have found the missing body. And I believe I can hazard a guess as to the identity of its killer."

"The Hirogen?" echoed Chakotay. "But that doesn't seem—"

"Logical?" said Tuvok, raising an eyebrow. "I could not agree with you more, Commander. And yet, the evidence is there."

Janeway sat frowning in her chair. The three were in her ready room, and she couldn't tear her eyes from the ghoulish spectacle of the small, furry Kuluuk body with no bones. She had little reason to like the Hirogen, after what one small group had done to her and her crew. She had no real reason to trust them. After all, as she had said earlier to this Alpha, it was a perfect opportunity for the Hirogen to add unique relics to their collections.

"The only reason we have not to believe it was the Hirogen is that their commander has given me his word that they wouldn't try anything like this," she said. "Otherwise, it's got their methods written all over it." Trying not to shudder, she placed down the padd with the image of the deboned Kuluuk on it. They had decided not to beam the body aboard, in the interests of not tampering further with the crime scene. Besides, there was little point in autopsying a body with no skeleton.

"We've got more than that," said Chakotay. "Think about the structure of Hirogen society. Think about the honor that's attached to their relics. What less impressive prey could there be for hunters who take such pride in their predatory prowess than a creature that keels over dead of fright? How could taking a relic from such prey confer any honor on its killer? And then trying to hide the crime, make it look like no killing had taken place at all. This doesn't ring true."

Janeway nodded. This had occurred to her as well.

"Also," continued Chakotay, "they positively boast of their kills. I don't think they'd make a false truce. They're too contemptuous to use trickery. If they wanted to kill us, they'd have tried openly." He shook his head. "This is not the way of the hunter, Captain. It's the way of the coward."

She didn't answer at once. Finally, she said, "I'm inclined to agree with you. It's obvious that the killer hoped we wouldn't notice that a murder had taken place at all. He—or she—wanted us to think the Kuluuk had died of natural causes. Just in case we were too smart to buy it, the killer had a backup plan: Place evidence that pointed to a specific species." She moved her arms in an exaggerated manner, accentuating her sarcasm. "Why, everyone knows the Hirogen are evil. Can't be trusted. They love to take trophies. No one is safe from them." Resuming her normal mien, she continued, "Except whoever did this doesn't know the Hirogen as well as we do. They'd target a species that would fight back—give them a challenge. They'd never try to cover up the killing. It's the cornerstone of their culture."

"What do you wish us to do now, Captain?" asked Tuvok.

Janeway didn't answer at once. What, indeed? All avenues would lead to strife, and few to answers. Even then she didn't know which one would be one of those few.

"I'm having trouble allaying suspicions as it is," she said. "There's nothing to stop any of the other species from scanning or beaming aboard the Kuluuk ship and finding things out for themselves. I've emphasized an openness with this group, a willingness to share food, supplies . . . information. If I keep ducking frank questions, it will only worsen the tension."

"If you tell the other ships that an entire crew contingent was murdered, and that all the circumstantial evidence points to the Hirogen, that certainly isn't going to decrease tension," said Chakotay.

"But it will increase confidence in Captain Janeway's policy of openness," Tuvok pointed out.

"And, unless there is some kind of conspiracy, there is probably only one species responsible for the deaths. The others would be anxious to clear their names, and quite possibly may offer more advanced technology for examining the ship."

"It's a lose-lose situation," Janeway said. "But the Kuluuk lost more than we ever will. We have to do everything possible to find their killers. All right. We've eliminated the Hirogen, even though the evidence points to them, because such a killing would be completely out of character with everything we know about them. Who else? Who had motivation? What could possibly be gained by slaughtering those people?"

"Someone could have wanted to frame the Hirogen. That might have been the entire purpose of the massacre. Certainly enough species have reason to hate them," said Chakotay.

Janeway shook her head. "That was my first thought, too. But if that had been the motive, there would have been no attempt to fool us into thinking that the Kuluuk had died of fright. The Hirogen angle was a backup, in case we saw through the first cover-up."

Tuvok raised an eyebrow and shifted in his seat. Immediately alert to even this subtle hint of discomfiture, Janeway asked, "What is it, Tuvok?"

"I am chagrined to admit that this had slipped my mind," said Tuvok, his voice harder than usual. "When I discovered the body, that took precedence."

"Of course," said Janeway, "but what is it you remember now?"

"The Kuluuk stores had been depleted. There was

no food remaining at all, yet they had no access to a replicator."

"But they were one of the few who never asked for help," said Janeway, seeing where Tuvok was going with this. "Chakotay, you had the most contact with them. What do you think? Was there some kind of deep-set pride that would have prevented them from asking for assistance when they were completely out of food?"

Chakotay shook his head. "Not at all. In fact, from what I knew about them, running low on supplies would have been something else that would have frightened them. They would have been embarrassed to ask for a handout, but fear was such a primal part of their makeup that they couldn't *not* ask if they were afraid. It's how they've survived. Their empire has always taken care of them."

"So I'm guessing that one of two things happened. Either they asked someone else for assistance, who transported into their ship and then killed them, or the killer was the one in need of assistance. He simply massacred the Kuluuk and helped himself to their stores."

"The Kuluuk were frightened enough about entering the nebula," said Chakotay. His face was sad as he recalled the last time he'd talked with the Kuluuk. "Getting through it safely would have been their top priority, as it was for everyone."

"Everyone except the killer," said Janeway, anger in her voice.

"They wouldn't be interested in a risky transport for supplies. That could easily have waited until they emerged on the other side."

"So. What do we have so far?" She took a sip of coffee. "We have seventeen representatives of non-Ku-luuk species who had been aboard that ship less than twenty-four hours before the massacre. One or per-haps more than one of those returned while the Ku-luuk were in the nebula, perhaps offering assistance. This person or persons broke Tarna's neck and fright-ened the rest to death. He, she, or they then gutted a corpse and stashed the body where it wouldn't be found at once, but could be found with diligent search-ing. This action was to point suspicion at the Hirogen, a race known for killing and taking trophies. Then, the killer or killers absconded with all the supplies they could take. Do I have it about right, gentlemen?"

They nodded.

"We can narrow the list of suspects down to the seventeen species who participated in the exchange program," said Tuvok. "We can eliminate the Hi-rogen for the reasons we've already discussed as well as any species that has adequate supplies."

"Unless the supplies were taken as yet another red herring," said Janeway. "A way to point suspicion to-ward someone other than the Hirogen."

"You're weaving a pretty tangled web, Captain," said Chakotay.

"Someone else wove it first," said Janeway. "Well, there's no point in prolonging this further. I'm going to call a meeting aboard *Voyager* and make the an-nouncement then."

It was worse than Janeway had imagined.

She had tried to do it as Tuvok would have, by giving a logical, unemotional presentation of the facts in the order in which they had been uncovered. She didn't even make it past "We were able to confirm that Captain Tarna's neck had been deliberately broken" when there was an uproar that drowned out the rest of her words.

"Murderers!" cried Torar, leaping up and pointing at a startled Kelmar. "It's got their cowardly stench all over it! It's not enough for you to attack my people and countless others, oh no, you've got to go and slay an entire ship of peaceful people who—"

"It's the Todanians!" someone else yelled, also rising to point a digit at an agitated and obviously offended Todanian representative, Akelm. "You see how little they regard other species' lives—they have slaves on their own ship!"

"The Willani were the last ones into the nebula after the Kuluuk," shouted Ellia. "They had the opportunity."

"What about the—"

"Silence!" cried Janeway. "No one is leaving this room until I have a chance to explain the entire situation!"

For several moments, it appeared as if the angry and highly stressed representatives of their various species were willing to accept staying in the room if it meant they could continue to argue and point fingers at one another. Janeway watched, feeling helpless. If the shouting matches escalated into fights, she could do something about it. But now, she had to get them quiet. They were not under her command, not really. They were all equals in this situation. They had to cooperate.

Finally, her repeated pleas for silence were

granted. Hoarse from shouting for the last ten minutes, she continued in a rough voice.

"I want everyone to be seated and be quiet until I have finished this," she said. "I am prepared to enforce that. Anyone who interrupts will be escorted out of this room. Is that clear?"

She saw nods, tentacle extensions, and claw snappings, and heard reluctant murmurs of agreement.

"Very good. Now, as I said, the captain of the Kuluuk was intentionally killed. It appears as though the others were terrorized to death. It's obvious that we were meant to think this whole thing was a tragic accident. Failing that, the killers left us clues to point to a particular species. I do not believe these clues to be true, but rather deliberately planted."

"Captain." It was an interruption, but a calm one. Janeway gazed, surprised, at the Hirogen Alpha. "Which species was made to look like the killer?"

"I'd rather not say at this point," said Janeway. Which was, apparently, the wrong thing to say. Chaos again erupted. Only when the security teams Tuvok had set up stepped into the center of the room and placed hands on the screaming aliens did even a hint of quiet return.

"Captain!" It was Ophar, hovering near the ceiling. "Captain, we have a right to know if there is a killer among us. You cannot withhold evidence. We must be able to defend ourselves. Who knows who will be the next target?"

Ophar's words, spoken calmly, pierced Janeway. She glanced uneasily at the Hirogen Alpha, then made her decision.

"I know you're all afraid," she said, as gently as

she could. "This is a frightening situation. But panic and rousing the mob mentality is not the answer. If any of you will let my teams board your vessel and examine it, it will exonerate you. We will be able to whittle down the suspects one by one."

"What about you, Captain?" Akelm said icily. "Will you permit a group of my crew to board *Voyager*, to scour its innards, and pronounce you safe?"

"Or my crew," said Kelmar. "We've no real reason to trust you, Captain. Any more than we have reason to trust anyone else." He glared at Ara and Torar, who glared right back.

"You agreed to accept *Voyager*'s leadership," began Janeway, wearily.

"And look where it got the Kuluuk," said Kelmar. Janeway was stung. "They trusted you to protect them. They put aside their fears and followed you into the nebula. They trusted someone you said they could trust, and now they are dead. You say the killers planted evidence to deflect suspicion. One of my crew was one of the seventeen aboard that ill-fated vessel. How do I know that you won't do the same to my ship? Make it look as though the Iudka are the heartless killers?"

"Iudka *are* heartless killers!" shrieked Ara.

"Or my ship," said Ellia, surprising and paining Janeway. "We have a trade agreement, Captain, nothing more. While we've been pleased to be part of this compact, I do not think it is in the best interests of my crew and my ship to let anyone, even someone from *Voyager*, board and search my vessel."

Janeway had opened her mouth to respond, when

her combadge chirped. "Chakotay to Janeway and Tuvok. We've just detected an unauthorized transport from the Todanian vessel to the Kuluuk ship."

Janeway closed her eyes briefly. All hell was about to break loose, and there wasn't anything she could do to prevent it. They'd left the deboned body on the ship, and it was only a matter of minutes before its horrors would be discovered. She locked gazes with Tuvok, all the way at the back of the room, and he nodded. Moving quickly and smoothly, he and his team moved toward the Hirogen entourage. They drew their phasers.

"Chakotay, get a lock on the Hirogen," Janeway ordered.

No sooner had she uttered the words than Akelm, who had been listening to one of his men, cried aloud. "The Hirogen!" he yelled, turning to point at them. "It was the Hirogen who killed the Kuluuk! We went aboard the ship and saw the body. It had no skeleton! The Hirogen took a relic!"

Janeway watched in horror as dozens of aliens, most of them decent, civilized people, began to shriek in anger. They moved toward the Hirogen in a vast, furious wave. Tuvok and his men closed in around the big, ugly aliens, their phasers pointed at the crowd.

"Transport the Hirogen to the brig," Janeway ordered. The forms of the Hirogen shimmered and disappeared. The crowd grew even more raucous, and the security team fired, their phasers set on a wide angle. Dozens fell where they stood. The gesture, fortunately, served to startle some sense back into those who remained. They froze in their tracks, clearly sullen and angry and resentful, but not manic, not anymore. They were the captains of their respective vessels, and while the situation was conducive to hysteria, they were intelligent enough to know when it was in their best interests not to offer a fight.

Janeway gasped for breath, staring at the diplomatic disaster before her eyes. At that moment, her badge chirped again.

"Chakotay to Janeway. I've got someone named Marisha who wants to talk to you."

"Not now, Chakotay," said Janeway, stepping down from the makeshift podium and hastening to her security chief. "You handle it."

"Kathryn," said Chakotay, and she stopped short at the use of her first name. "Marisha is a V'enah. Apparently, there has been a slave revolt on the *Relka*. She's requesting asylum."

CHAPTER

15

JANEWAY MADE HER DECISION. THE ASSEMBLED GROUP
was either unconscious or under control, for the moment. The Hirogen were safe in the brig, where no
angry mob could reach them.

"On my way," she told Chakotay. As she sprinted
for the door, she called out over her shoulder, "Keep
them here until I return, Tuvok."

Never had it seemed to take so long for Janeway
to reach the bridge. The minute the door hissed
open, she looked up at the screen and snapped, "Tell
me what's going on, Marisha."

It was her first look at a V'enah. Thin and with
skin and hair colored in hues of purple from soft
pastel lavender to deep violet, the woman bent over
the tiny viewscreen in the small escape pod. She had
dark purple hair that was cut extremely short and in

a choppy manner. She would have been pretty, had she had some softening flesh to her angular skull. Marisha was highly agitated and her face was flushed as she spoke.

"We need asylum!" she screamed, her face looming huge on the screen. "Please, Captain, what we have seen of your crew makes me believe that we can trust you. We need your help!"

"What happened? I heard something about an uprising. Did you lead an attack? How many are dead?"

"We didn't kill anyone," said Marisha. "We just wanted to get out. Seven of Nine told us we should leave and she was right."

Janeway tensed. Was Seven responsible, directly or indirectly, for this uprising? "I read her report. The conditions aboard your ship are deplorable and I sympathize with your plight. But I won't support a violent uprising. Tell me exactly what happened."

"Grant us asylum!" Marisha cried, tears welling in her eyes. Janeway saw cuts and bruises on the purple skin and fresh blood on her outfit. Whatever had happened, the V'enah hadn't simply sneaked away in the middle of the night.

An insistent beeping caught her attention. "It's the *Relka*," said Kim. "Arkathi wants to talk to you."

"*No!*" Marisha's eyes widened. "No, Captain, do not listen to him! He is Todanian, he lies—"

Her face disappeared from the screen. In its place was the image of six small escape pods being fired upon by the massive Todanian ship. Even as Janeway watched, one of them exploded into flames.

"Shields up! Get a tractor beam on those pods!"

Janeway yelled. "Open a channel. Janeway to Arkathi. Hold your fire or we will fire in return!"

Her words had no effect. The *Relka* fired again, narrowly missing another pod.

"Kim, get them as close as you can. The minute it's possible, extend our shields to protect them. Chakotay," she said to her first officer, who stood at Tuvok's post, "fire a warning shot. If they attack again, we do too."

"Aye, Captain," said Chakotay. Red energy sliced across the *Relka*'s bow but did no damage.

"They're targeting us," said Kim. Hardly had the words escaped his mouth when the ship rocked violently. Janeway dug her fingers into the chair arms and hung on. Chakotay didn't need the order repeated; he fired upon the *Relka*.

"Their weapons are temporarily disabled," he reported.

"Open a channel," Janeway ordered.

The unattractive, angry visage of Sinimar Arkathi filled the screen. "I demand that you return my property!"

"They have asked for asylum," said Janeway, fighting to maintain her cool. "From what I've seen, they are indeed in danger. What did they do, Arkathi?"

He stared, then broke into harsh laughter. "Do? Why, they killed, Captain! They killed fifteen people! If you don't recognize our right to the V'enah as property, then at least you will understand why we want to bring murderers to justice!"

That seemed to be the prevailing theme over the last few hours, Janeway thought. "We will incarcerate them on our vessel until we can get to the bottom of this."

The swiftness of his movement startled even her. Snarling, he sprang from his command chair and pressed his face into the viewscreen. His red throat sacs inflated as he spoke. "You will return our property to us for execution!"

"You will sit down and let justice take its course," said Janeway, her icy softness a sharp contrast to Arkathi's raging. "We've lost the Ammunii vessel, and now we've lost entire crew of the *Eru*. I won't add more body counts to those we already have. Janeway out."

She turned to look at Chakotay, still standing at Tuvok's post. "Don't talk to him anymore, not for now. If they start getting itchy fingers, you're under orders to return fire for fire, but nothing more. I want to do nothing that could escalate this situation. Harry, are those pods in the shuttle bay yet?"

"Just docking now," said Kim.

"Have Seven and a security team meet them and escort them to sickbay. I'm going to talk to the Hirogen." She rose and strode to the turbolift, pondering what Seven's role in all of this might have been. If she had indeed been responsible for bloodshed, she had a lot to answer for.

Seven of Nine kept her emotions from showing on her face as she and a security team "escorted" the escaped V'enah to sickbay. No one was so seriously injured he couldn't walk, but neither was any member of that group without damage of some sort.

Marisha looked over at her several times, but took

her own cue from Seven's demeanor. It was only when all of the V'enah, a small handful of only eleven, were in sickbay and being treated by the Doctor that the alleged leader of the alleged revolt spoke.

"We are grateful that your captain has granted us asylum," she said.

"Captain Janeway has ordered you confined to the brig until the matter has been thoroughly investigated," Seven corrected her. "She has not yet granted you anything but safety."

Marisha smiled sadly. "Our injuries will be treated. We will have sufficient food and water. We will not be forced to perform brutal labor and left to rot where we fall. To me, this is asylum, no matter what term you use."

Seven could think of no proper response to that. She struggled to keep her gaze from wandering to Marisha's, but it was impossible. Something about the other woman had captivated her soul, and Seven knew she would not be released from that bond until she had done everything she could to help Marisha. Help her people.

"Leader Arkathi claims you killed in order to effect your escape. Is this true?"

Marisha's eyes narrowed and her breathing quickened. "We fought, yes; that much is true. My orders were to have the weapons on low. I cannot vouch for every action taken by every V'enah who escaped with me, but I certainly did not wish to kill and I gave instructions to that effect. We would be no better than the Todanians if we did that. I would not knowingly start my life of freedom with blood on my hands."

"I believe you," said Seven firmly. "I will be your advocate."

Marisha smiled, slowly, hesitantly. The smile grew until she was almost radiant with it. Seven knew she was doing the right thing, regardless of what Janeway might order.

"The evidence is overwhelming," stated the Hirogen Alpha in a calm voice. "Nonetheless, we did not do it."

His second was less composed. "Massacre a race of cowards? The accusation in itself is an insult!"

"Besides," said the Alpha, lifting a hand to signal his subordinate to be silent, "we promised that we would abide by the agreement we made with you. There is no honor in dissolving that agreement, especially not for such pathetic relics."

"We believe you," said Janeway, and she could see that she surprised them. "We think you've been made to look like the killers, when in reality someone else has done the killing. We are willing to do what we can to prove your innocence."

The Alpha nodded, as if what she had just said had merely been what he had expected. "If it will help, you may search our vessel and report the findings to all the others in the caravan."

"That's a start," said Janeway. "There are seventeen species, including mine and yours, who were on that vessel and who will start our list of suspects. We're eliminating you, and by that gesture, I think you can agree to eliminate us."

The Alpha inclined his head. "If you had set us up as the main suspects, you would hardly now try to demonstrate our innocence."

"Fifteen races, then. Commander Tuvok will continue to work with you." She rose. "I've got Chakotay on the bridge trying to manage all those other people who are convinced you did it. And I've also got a slave uprising on my hands, with fifteen people dead. If you'll excuse me."

Janeway nodded to the security guard posted at the brig's entrance and frowned at the sight that met her gaze. Seven of Nine was inside the cell with Marisha. They were sitting close to each other, heads bent close in intense conversation. The contrast was striking—Seven's full head of blond hair almost touching Marisha's purple, shorn scalp; her full, curved figure seated beside the V'enah's nearly skeletal frame. But they were both tall, strong women, and when they paused in their conversation to turn and regard Janeway, they looked more alike than dissimilar.

"Seven, a moment." She deactivated the forcefield and Seven stepped out of the cell. Janeway walked a few feet away, then said in a quiet voice, "Marisha said you urged them to an uprising. The Doctor commented to me on some of your more inappropriate comments while the two of you were on the *Relka*. Your own report is full of passion and outrage for the V'enah's plight, something I don't ordinarily hear from you. Now I find you sitting side by side, talking so softly that neither the guard nor I can hear you. So tell me. What am I supposed to be thinking, Seven?"

Seven tilted her chin up defiantly. "That I am interested in justice and freedom."

Janeway searched her gaze, then sighed. "Chakotay said that you'd be able to identify with the V'enah, as you were in a similar situation."

"From which you yourself liberated me," said Seven.

"True. But that was—" Janeway suddenly realized how it sounded and stopped.

"Different?" Seven finished. "How? I would say that this is a worse situation. These people are able to comprehend how badly they are being treated. Drones cannot. You see what they have done to her."

"And I hear what they have done to their captors. According to Arkathi, fifteen people are dead."

"Arkathi is not telling the truth," said Seven, with the firmness of one stating an absolute fact, not an opinion. Janeway raised an eyebrow.

"Really? I want you to come with me, Seven. Arkathi has asked us to see the carnage for ourselves."

"Marisha did not do it."

"Seven, perhaps she individually didn't. But someone killed these people. Let's go."

Seven hesitated, then threw a glance over her shoulder at Marisha, as if asking the other woman's permission. Marisha stood as close as possible to the forcefield.

"Go with her, Seven," Marisha said, her voice ringing with conviction. "We are innocent. Go and see for yourself."

A few moments later, Seven and Janeway, tricorders in hand and phasers at their hips, materialized in the transporter room of the *Relka*. Seven realized that her body was tense, as if expecting an assault.

"Captain Janeway. Seven of Nine," said Sinimar Arkathi, in the most pleasant tone Seven had yet heard from him. Janeway, too, seemed surprised at his pleasant demeanor. "Thank you for coming. I have instructed my security to leave everything untouched. It is all as we found it, in all its brutal detail. You should brace yourselves."

"We're veterans of battle, Leader," said Janeway icily. "You won't be showing us anything we haven't seen."

"We'll see about that. May I point out the blood where you are standing," said Arkathi. Seven looked down. Sure enough, she was standing in a pool of thick yellow liquid. A few drops of purple liquid were scattered around as well. She turned on the tricorder and began recording. "Mostly Todanian blood, but I am pleased to admit that not all the blood spilled belonged to us."

Seven set her jaw. She followed her captain, who carefully glanced around. "I thought the V'enah fled in the escape pods," she said.

"They did, but only because we had put a lock on the transporters," Arkathi replied. "They came here first and discovered there was no escape this way. Please, follow me. It's a grisly tour of my ship you'll be taking."

They followed him, while he pointed out spatters of blood here and there. They turned a corner and Arkathi held up a hand to stop them. "Proceed carefully," he said.

The two humans turned the corner and gazed at the first body. It was a Todanian security guard. He lay facedown in a pool of viscous yellow fluid. A hole had been blasted into his torso. Seven resisted the impulse to cover her nose from the rising stench.

"There are two more," said Arkathi, pointing down the corridor. Two more security guards lay where they had fallen. Seven stared, wanting to disbelieve. Marisha wouldn't have done this, *couldn't* have done it. She knew it, and yet there the evidence lay. Arkathi turned and headed down another corridor, away from the bodies. Janeway followed. After a moment, Seven, feeling dazed, followed as well.

More bodies. And now, to her horror, Seven began to see the corpses not only of Arkathi guards—which Marisha and her people could conceivably have attacked in self-defense—but of unarmed workers.

"These three were unfortunate enough to be returning from their duty shift to their quarters," said Arkathi, his voice harsh. "They could have offered no real threat to armed slaves, yet the V'enah scum slew them regardless."

Seven felt her captain's eyes boring into her. Janeway didn't need to say anything; Seven could all but hear the conversation in her mind: *We've seen nine bodies so far, Seven. Nine. Marisha said she didn't kill anyone. Yet she was the leader; she had to have known that these people died. What do you say now? How can you stand by her claim that she is innocent?*

Seven could not recall feeling so miserable in her life. How could this be so? How could Marisha, who had so quickly managed to get into Seven's mind and heart, be a cold-blooded killer? And yet the bodies spoke volumes, though their voices were forever silenced.

On they went, tracking a trail of slaughter. Civilians would have been appalled and nauseated by the sight and stench. Even Seven, who was no stranger to carnage, and Janeway, who Seven knew had seen battle intimately, could not help but react.

"This is the worst," said Arkathi as they stood before a large door. "This is engineering, where the leader of the uprising was stationed. This is where it began." The door slid open to reveal eight corpses.

Seven's blue eyes widened and her full lips trembled.

Arkathi was right. This was the worst, because the dead here were not armed guards, nor even unarmed Todanians. The only people to have died in here, where Marisha had been a slave, were her fellow V'enah.

"Personally, I do not care about their worthless lives," said Arkathi. "But the thought that any sentient creature, even a V'enah, would so ruthlessly slaughter its own species for its freedom . . . well, you may not think highly of me, Captain, but even I am sickened by this."

Seven felt as though she were walking in a living nightmare. She stepped over the bodies. Thin, pale purple, their eyes had been wide with shock and surprise as they had died. She thought she recognized a few. There was Talyk, the man who had taken the wrong turn and been beaten for his "transgression." There was a woman she remembered, a youth who had smiled at her despite a mouthful of broken teeth when she treated him.

No. No, she could not have been so mistaken. This was wrong. Something was wrong, though she did not know what, but this was not what it seemed, it couldn't be. . . .

"Seven," said Janeway, grasping the former Borg's upper arm gently to steady her. "Let's return to the ship. I think we've seen enough."

Seven licked her lips and straightened, forcing composure on a body that wanted nothing more than to curl up in a fetal position and shudder with the shock of betrayal. "Of course, Captain," she said, keeping her voice as steady as possible.

"Now, you understand," said Arkathi. "You can see why we want to bring the woman who did this and those who obeyed her brutal orders to justice."

"I do, Commander," said Janeway. "My apologies for doubting you."

Unexpectedly, Arkathi seemed to soften. He waved her words aside. "We have clashed in the past, you and I. But that is forgotten. We need to bring the V'enah and the Hirogen to justice. Then our caravan can move on with, I hope, less friction."

Seven said nothing. She remained silent the entire way back to the transporter room. When she and Janeway materialized on *Voyager,* Janeway ushered her out of the room. Alone in the corridor, Janeway said softly, with great compassion, "Seven, I'm sorry. I didn't want to believe it either. Regardless of how dreadful an institution slavery is, we can't let slaves win their freedom by murdering their captors."

Seven did not answer, nor did she meet her captain's eyes.

"Seven?"

"I believed her," Seven said in a low, husky voice. "I believed her when she said that they would be no better than the Todanians if they stooped to murder."

Janeway's face grew soft. Gently, she placed a hand on Seven's shoulder. "I know. I wanted to, too. It fits with what we think is right and just. And in a way, it's hard to blame Marisha. What kind of a life must she have led? How in the world could she possibly learn a real moral code when—"

Seven stiffened. She stared at the tricorder in her hand as if it were a lifeline. "Captain, please don't authorize the transfer of the V'enah to the *Relka* immediately."

"I don't think it's a good idea for you to have any further conversation with Marisha," said Janeway. "Don't make me make it an order."

"No, that's not it. Something is incorrect, out of proper alignment. I . . . I feel that there may be something we're overlooking."

Janeway raised an eyebrow and smiled. "Why, Seven," she said, a hint of mirth in her voice, "are you having a hunch?"

Seven returned the smile, though it felt forced. "I believe you may be correct, Captain. Please. A half hour is all I need to verify this . . . hunch."

"All right. I'll stall Arkathi. But that's all. Believe me, if you can find something, anything, that can be construed as solid evidence to exonerate the V'enah, I'll support you."

"Thank you, Captain." It was all Seven could do not to break into a run as she headed toward the turbolift. "Sickbay," she told it, and the speedy transportation device had never seemed so slow to her.

"Doctor," she said, preempting any greeting he might give, "did you record every patient we examined on the *Relka?*"

"And hello to you too," he said, a trifle annoyed. "Of course. Why?"

"I need to review the information immediately."

He gazed at her, his dark eyes searching hers, then went to his station. He tapped the controls, then rose and indicated that she take the chair. "Here it is. It begins when we transported down and continues through the last person treated. Have fun."

She ignored the gibe and slid into the seat. Something caught her attention and she glanced up. On the Doctor's desk was a small bowl of water containing an orange fish. The fish floated, unmoving, at the surface.

"Doctor, your fish has expired."

"Damn! Computer, delete hologram." The image of the bowl with the floating fish vanished.

"To what purpose was there a fish in sickbay?" Seven asked.

The Doctor sighed. "Just an experiment, that's all. One that went awry. I'd, um, appreciate it if you wouldn't mention this to the captain."

Seven raised an eyebrow. "Very well," she agreed, then turned her attention to the task at hand. Swiftly she began to scan the scene the tricorder had recorded. She saw herself and the Doctor preparing the rations. The Todanians were the first to be treated. Seven heard again her own voice giving instructions, Arkathi's rude remarks. Arkathi grew angry and stalked out of the room.

The Doctor began treating the Todanians. The first was as arrogant as his captain, but the second was much more polite. "You are kind to help us," he told the Doctor. Seven started. She now recognized him as one of the unarmed Todanians who had been on his way to his quarters when he had been killed. A quick glance at the recording she had just made aboard the *Relka* confirmed it.

"Computer, edit and recompile all data on this individual," she instructed. An instant later, the computer told her, "Task completed."

She watched all the Todanians receive treatment and food. And she saw herself begin showing signs of irritation with the assignment.

"Let me guess, Seven. You feel like your time and unique talents are being wasted on this assignment," said the recorded image of the Doctor.

"Correct," said the recorded Seven.

"So do I. Anyone could administer these vitamin supplements and rehydration hypos. I haven't even seen so much as a scratch on any of them. The Todanians are almost obscenely healthy. Some of them could stand to skip a few meals."

"Seven of Nine to Commander Chakotay." Seven watched as she attempted to neglect her duty, and felt shame heating her face. She knew now, as she had not then, what was to come.

"This is Chakotay. How's it going?"

"Inefficiently," Seven replied. "They have isolated us in a cargo bay and are sending the Todanians in for treatment and food. I request to be relieved of this assignment."

"Me too," said the Doctor.

"As does the Doctor. There's nothing—"

And Seven saw her own eyes go wide, her mouth open in surprise. The V'enah were entering.

She again saw the guards attack an unarmed man, heard herself order them to stand aside. She saw

Marisha try to appear subservient, but caught anew the flicker of defiance in the V'enah woman's eyes. Seven knew now that this woman could never have planned or executed the carnage she had witnessed on the *Relka*. And she was about to prove it.

The Doctor on the recording leaped into action. Seven saw again how the V'enah regarded Marisha with deference.

"They are here to help us," said the recorded Marisha. "Do what they tell you to."

Seven fast-forwarded through her treatment of Marisha. She wasn't the one Seven was interested in. Not this time.

"We operate the heavy machinery," said Marisha. "It is one of the more dangerous tasks aboard the ship."

"Yes," said Seven, aloud. "Yes, it is dangerous."

They were talking about the food now. "There is not that much," said Seven, treating another woman. The Seven of the present leaned forward eagerly. This was what she had wanted to see. "According to our estimates, that is the standard amount of calories and nutrients you should be consuming per day."

"We get about a third of this," said the woman Seven was treating. "I get more. Arkathi gives it to me and I steal what he does not eat off his plate."

"You serve Arkathi?" asked Seven on the tricorder.

"I am his personal servant. I am Kella. I have not seen the others before now. I didn't know how badly . . . Are you done?"

"Computer, freeze image."

She stared intently at Kella. At the soft skin, the

rounded flesh, the pretty clothes, the clean hair and body.

Kella was Arkathi's personal servant.

Kella had never labored a single day in engineering.

So why had Seven seen Kella lying dead, supposedly murdered by Marisha, in the most physically demanding section of the entire ship?

"Seven to Captain Janeway," she said, and there was pride and relief in her voice. "I have found the evidence you requested."

CHAPTER
16

"Seven, I hate to disappoint you, but I don't know how solid this evidence of yours is," said Janeway.

"Kella was a personal servant of Arkathi," Seven said, hammering at the information that Janeway already knew. "She had never even encountered the V'enah who performed the hard labor. She was fed well, clothed well . . . look at her in comparison to Marisha."

Janeway had, but to make Seven feel as though she had been heard, she looked again at the corpse Seven had indicated on the tricorder. Kella lay sprawled in a pool of her own purple blood. Her figure, while not fat, was curved and feminine. One hand was upturned, and Janeway saw there was no hint of a callus on it. Peering closer, she saw that the dead woman had even worn cosmetics. The clothes she wore looked new.

"I'll grant you that Kella looks out of place among the other V'enah," said Janeway. "But who's to say that she wasn't recently assigned there? You know Arkathi, Seven. Perhaps she had done something to offend him, and he wanted to teach her a lesson. Then she would simply have been in the wrong place at the wrong time."

Seven stepped in beside her captain and tapped the tricorder. "Kella is still wearing cosmetics," she pointed out. "Do you think Arkathi would have allowed that if he wanted, as you say, to teach her a lesson? He would have stripped her of everything that reminded her of her previous rank. She would never have been allowed to have anything that made her feel beautiful or different from the other slaves."

Unease stirred inside Janeway. Maybe Seven was on to something. "I hadn't considered that. Good detective work, Seven."

"And this man, a Todanian." Taking the tricorder from Janeway, Seven called up another image. "He expressed embarrassment at the way Arkathi was behaving. This woman was friendly to us. Don't you find it interesting that all the dead Todanians are ones who seemed to disagree, even mildly, with Arkathi's way of doing things? Captain, this may not be enough to convict in a court of law, but you must agree with me that it raises questions that we must have answered before we can in good conscience turn the V'enah over to Arkathi's so-called justice."

Janeway nodded. "We'll confront him with what you've found and see how he reacts. If he transferred

Kella, then he should have records to show us." Her blue eyes flashed in anticipation. "I wouldn't mind watching him squirm a bit. I've got another idea as well. Janeway to Tuvok."

"Tuvok here, Captain."

"I need you to do a little research for me. And keep it quiet."

Sinimar Arkathi was already on the viewscreen, larger than life, arguing with Chakotay when Janeway and Seven stepped onto the bridge.

"There you are. What are you waiting for, Captain? Hand over our prisoners immediately."

"Not quite yet, Commander." Janeway tried to smile pleasantly as she sank into her command chair. Seven stood rigidly at attention beside her. "I've got a few questions. My sharp-eyed crew member noticed a few things when we were aboard your ship."

Arkathi's throat sacs inflated so greatly that Janeway wondered if they would explode. The thought didn't bother her much.

"Captain Janeway," he said, in a cold and tightly controlled voice, "you have the prisoners who admit that they used our weapons against us. You have seen the trail of slaughter they left in their escape. What more do you require of us? I think we have been very patient—"

"And if you'll continue to be patient for about three more minutes, we could solve this," said Janeway, an edge creeping into her voice despite her best efforts. She glanced down at the padd. "One of the V'enah found slain was identified by Marisha as your personal servant Kella. Is this true?"

She watched him closely, but the comment didn't appear to unnerve him. "She's lying. How would she even know such a thing?"

"Seven of Nine met Kella and Marisha both on the day she and the Doctor transported aboard your vessel to treat your injured," said Janeway. "Kella identified herself as such. Marisha merely confirmed what Seven already knew."

Now he did look slightly uncomfortable. "So? What is your point, Captain?"

"Kella's body was not found in a corridor, but in engineering. Dressed in working clothes, as if that was her usual station."

"I transferred her there. I am allowed to do what I want with my property, Captain."

The anger boiled in her so hotly that she had to force it down. She continued in a calm voice, "Then may I see the records?"

He became very still. "To what end?"

"To prove what you've just told me. That you transferred your personal servant to engineering."

"There are no records. I did it in a moment of rashness. It was not a permanent transfer. You can imagine my chagrin at discovering that my own personal servant was among the victims of this terrible tragedy."

"Actually, I can't," said Janeway. "Why didn't you tell us sooner? It would have made us even more sympathetic."

"I don't have to justify myself to you!" He was spitting his words now.

Janeway leaned forward in her chair, her gaze locked on Arkathi. "And don't you find it interesting that all the Todanians killed by the escaping slaves were ones who had expressed sympathy for the V'enah? Who had perhaps made comments about your poor leadership?"

"I refuse to continue this charade. You have both the murderous slaves and the Hirogen on your ship, yet you sit here and attack me as if I were the one under suspicion!"

"You are," said Janeway, icily. "Tuvok, what were the results of that research I had you do?"

"Positive, Captain," the Vulcan replied. "I detected traces of Kuluuk supplies aboard the *Relka*."

"Interesting," Janeway purred, feeling like the cat with the mouse. "I seem to recall an argument with you in which you complained that your rations were running out and demanded more. Perhaps you'd care to tell us how those came to be aboard your ship?"

"They were gifts, after our visit," said Arkathi.

No. They were not.

The voice was as loud, as clear, as if it had been shouted, but Janeway heard it only in her head. She whirled to see a small, slight figure standing next to the turbolift. Tuvok immediately trained a phaser on the intruder.

More quickly than spoken words, information flooded Janeway's mind. She guessed by the reaction of Arkathi and the rest of her bridge crew that they too could understand the stranger.

Arkathi murdered the Kuluuk. Their ship suffered another power drain and they were dead in space. The Relka *came upon them and offered assistance. Arkathi murdered Tarna, and the rest died of fright, as you have surmised. Arkathi did not think anyone would suspect, as the Kuluuk are known to be so fragile. Nonetheless, he removed the skeleton of one Kuluuk, disintegrated it, and hid the body where a careful search would discover it, so if suspicions were raised, it would appear as if the Hirogen had committed the atrocity.*

He lied to his crew, telling them that he had accidentally frightened the entire ship to death, and reasoned that the Todanians should take the supplies rather than letting them go to waste. When it was revealed that the captain had been murdered, some of his crew began to suspect and voiced their disapproval.

So Arkathi had to silence them. Marisha's escape attempt was the perfect opportunity. He slew all the V'enah in her area, so they would not speak in favor of their leader, and killed his personal servant as well, who had been displeasing him recently. Those of his own people who had spoken out against him were also slain. He had perfect . . . what is your term . . . scapegoats, Captain, but the blood of dozens is on his hands.

"Who are you?" Arkathi demanded. "Why are you telling these lies?"

The being turned to face the viewscreen. *I am Leader of the Ones Who Will Not Be Named. We have been following this caravan since its inception, watching everything. We have records of all your crimes, Arkathi, and though it goes against our very beings to come forward with this information, we could not remain silent and see so many die without justice.*

She didn't know how she knew it, but Janeway knew in her bones that this mysterious being who had manifested on her ship was telling the truth. Tuvok had once said something along the lines that there could be no lies in a telepathic link. She believed it now.

And judging by Arkathi's reaction, he knew it to be the truth as well. For the first time since she had met him, he cast aside even the veneer of culture. He hunched forward and made an incomprehensible, snarling sound, then abruptly terminated conversation.

"Their shields are up," said Tuvok.

"Get ours up too," said Janeway, and not a moment too soon. The ship rocked from the *Relka*'s attack. Before Janeway could even open her mouth, a second volley came. And a third.

"They're trying to blast us to bits," cried Chakotay.

"Fire," gasped Janeway, but before Tuvok could obey, the *Relka* was struck by green phaser fire and, a moment later, by photon torpedoes.

"It's the *Umul* and the *Nivvika*," said Chakotay. "They've come to our aid."

"Tom, pattern beta theta alpha," Janeway ordered. Obediently Paris put the ship through its maneuvers. More ships were closing in, firing at Arkathi's vessel. Even as Janeway watched, the Nenlars, in their tiny ship, approached. It was an act, she knew, that had taken tremendous courage.

She didn't believe in premonitions, but she knew that ship was going to be in trouble. "Kim, open a channel to the Nenlars. They've got to get out of—"

The *Relka* fired. The Nenlar vessel went reeling.

Janeway watched in horror as it turned end over end, then exploded. There hadn't even been time for her to get a lock on Ara and Torar. Grief welled in her, but another volley from the *Relka* quickly forced her to lay aside any mourning she might do.

They were taking a beating. It was as if now, with no chance of escaping justice, Arkathi was determined to drag *Voyager* down with him. Then all at once, the firing stopped.

"Harry, raise the *Relka.*"

"They're beating us to it, Captain."

"Onscreen."

It took her a moment to recognize the young, rather frightened-looking male Todanian whose image filled the bridge's viewscreen. Then she placed him: he was Sook, the fourth of Arkathi's retinue to dine with her that evening. The one who had looked back, embarrassed, when his commander stormed out. . . .

"Captain Janeway?" he asked, and the translator confirmed her suspicions that this was a youth.

"Yes. Where's Arkathi?"

"We don't know. He ran. We're trying to stop him but he's barricaded himself in the pod bay and has overridden all the controls. We only just got visual back. Captain, please don't keep firing on us. We don't believe in what Arkathi did. We're trying to catch him ourselves."

He speaks the truth, came Leader's "voice" in Janeway's mind. She had come to the same conclusion herself.

"We'll withhold fire," she agreed, "but if—"

"Sook!" The young Todanian whirled at the sound

of his name. Someone Janeway couldn't see was calling to him. "He's gotten in one of the escape pods."

"Put a tractor beam on it!" Sook cried.

"We can't!" the unseen Todanian yelled back. "It's still offline!"

"Perhaps we can help," said Janeway. "On main screen." Sure enough, there it was, a single small pod fleeing into space. "Tuvok, can you get him?"

"I will attempt—" The lights flickered. They returned for a moment, flickered again, and went out. The emergency lighting came on and the bridge was bathed in a bloody glow.

"What the hell was that?" She turned to look at Leader. "Is this your doing?"

The small being gestured impotently. *The power drain is affecting all our ships. We believe that it's coming from the gateways themselves. That they are fueling themselves with our power. Masters Technology has been working on it and we have learned all that you have about it, but no one seems to know how to stop it.*

"Captain," said Chakotay. "You'd better look at this." He touched a control, and instead of Sinimar Arkathi's escape pod, the viewscreen now showed all the various gateways that had been their silent, mysterious, softly glowing companions on this bizarre journey.

Except now, they weren't softly glowing. Even as she watched, enthralled and horrified at the same time, each doorway in the sky exploded with color. Before she ducked her head to shield her vision, she saw every color of the rainbow, and then some. It was a glorious, dazzling display.

She blinked, forcing her nearly blinded gaze to refocus, and inhaled swiftly.

The gateways were gone.

The ship was dead.

And Sinimar Arkathi's escape pod was nowhere to be seen.

CHAPTER

17

THERE WAS A HARSH CRACKLE, AND THEN THE LIGHTS that indicated the forcefields were operative blinked off. The security guard immediate lifted his phaser.

"Don't move," he warned. The V'enah exchanged glances. Many of them turned to Marisha. She rose, went to the forcefield, and extended a hand. Simultaneously, the guard fired.

Nothing. Neither from the guard's phaser or the forcefield.

They could leave if they wanted to. She heard laughter and some of the V'enah surged forward. Whirling, she extended her hands.

"No," she cried.

"Marisha, the field is down and the guard's weapon is inoperative! It's our chance!" one of them yelled.

"No. Our chance lies with Captain Janeway and

217

Seven. The eleven of us can't take this entire ship. We stay where we are and hope for justice." Slowly, she turned to face the guard. "You see how we trust your captain," she said. "I hope you—*look out!*"

Her warning came too late. The Hirogen had none of the compunctions that Marisha had. They left their cells, struck the guard with a casual blow that was nonetheless quite sufficient to render him unconscious, and moved toward the doors without a word. They did not open, but the two huge aliens forced their way through with ease.

Marisha watched them go. She closed her eyes and hoped she was doing the right thing.

"What just happened?" Janeway demanded. "Seven—I need you in astrometrics. See if you can find any gateways in this sector."

Seven nodded her blond head and headed for the turbolift, not without a backward glance at Leader. It was that last glance that caused her to slam right into the door that refused to open.

"The doors are offline," she said, trying to maintain her dignity. "I will utilize the Jefferies tube."

"Hurry, Seven. Tuvok, any comments?"

"Inconclusive. Any statement I might make at this juncture would be considered mere conjecture," said Tuvok, maddeningly Vulcan.

"Leader," said Janeway. "Do you know anything that might help us?"

Leader hesitated, then sent, *I will return to my vessel and send One Who Masters Technology and One Who Braves Strangers to speak with Chief Engineer Torres.* And just that quickly, he was gone.

No hum of a transporter, nothing . . . he simply vanished.

"Now *that* was odd," said Paris dryly.

"Torres, prepare for visitors. It's difficult to explain, but I think they're allies."

"They're already here, Captain," said Torres, her voice sounding tight over the comlink. "I'll let you know what we find."

"Ensign Harris to Janeway. The Hirogen have escaped."

"Explain," snapped Janeway.

"When that power surge happened, the forcefields went down and my phaser wouldn't operate. The V'enah stayed put, but the Hirogen came up behind me." There was a bit of self-disgust in his voice, but Janeway knew that no one on her crew would have been able to stop the Hirogen without a weapon.

"Acknowledged. Tuvok, issue a shipwide alert. Without power, they won't get too far. Kim, get Sook back."

After a moment, Kim shook his dark head. "I can't, Captain. Everything's down. And from what I can tell, all the other ships in our caravan have suffered the same fate."

Mr. Kim is right, came Leader's thoughts in Janeway's mind. *The doorways have closed, but not before they drained the energy in every ship.*

Janeway couldn't believe it. She felt stunned. They were all dead in the water, to borrow a several-hundred-year-old phrase, and there didn't appear to be a damn thing she could do about it.

"Well," said Chakotay, breaking the silence, "at least no one's firing at us anymore."

"I wonder what happened to Arkathi," said Janeway. "I suppose we'll never know." She took a deep breath. "Torres, how are you and our friends coming along?"

"I'd kill for an axe along about now," said Torres. "When they said everything is out, they meant everything is out. Phasers, everything. All but the emergency lighting."

"Keep working on it, Torres. Life support needs to be the main thing. If—"

There was another flash of rainbow light. Again, Janeway hissed in pain and lifted a hand to shield her eyes from the shining glare. And as suddenly as they had gone off, the lights came back on again. The panels flashed to life, and the subtle, oft ignored but now very welcomed hums of a ship running at full power reached Janeway's ears. Blinking, Janeway stared at the screen.

"They're back," she said aloud. They had only shut down for about ten minutes, and now they were reactivated.

"Security to bridge. We have apprehended the Hirogen."

And as if the ship's return to power had fueled her as well, Janeway began issuing orders. "Good work. Take them back to the brig. Janeway to the caravan. A short distance away, there is a small class-M planet. We need to make for it at once. The gateways may be in their last stages of operation and could shut down permanently at any time, and we've all seen what that could do to us. We need to be near a habitable planet, in the event that we need to evacuate. We will be sending you the coordinates. Please utilize your vessel's top speed to rendezvous in orbit. If anyone needs a tow, please request it now."

She waited for several ships to pipe up; no one did. A quick scan confirmed that all the ships were back to, if not full power, then at least adequate power to reach the planet. "According to my data, it looks like we'll all be able to make it. We will speak again once we are all in orbit around the planet." She hesitated, then said, "Godspeed. Janeway out." She glanced over at Kim. "Ensign," she began, but Kim interrupted her.

"Coordinates sent, Captain."

"Good job, Harry. Tom—"

"Course laid in, Captain. Ready to move at warp nine when you give the signal."

She smiled. "Consider it given," she said. "Nice to know my crew's on top of things."

Marisha was asleep when Janeway approached her cell. All of the V'enah were, curled up together in a small pile, their arms wrapped around each other as if offering support and reassurance even in sleep. For a moment Janeway stood, then finally spoke.

"Marisha," she said, just loudly enough to wake her. Marisha opened her eyes; then, as one, the V'enah started awake, frightened looks on their faces. "I'm sorry. I tried not to startle you. I understand you opted not to escape. I thank you for your confidence in me."

"Captain." She was completely awake now, her painfully thin body tense, as if ready to jump. "What is it?" Fear flickered across her face. "Are you returning us to the *Relka* for judgment?"

"No," Janeway replied, smiling. "Far from it. You're free." As quickly as she could, Janeway told

Marisha about Seven's discoveries and their confrontation of Arkathi. Marisha and the others, crowding around their leader, listened intently as she described the timely and peculiar appearance of the leader of the Ones Who Will Not Be Named, the strange shutdown of the doorways and the dire consequences, the equally strange resumption of gateway activity, and the class-M planet to which every ship in the caravan was heading at top speed.

"I regret to inform you that when the gateways flared, we were distracted. We lost sight of Arkathi's escape pod. We scanned the area, but we had no success locating him or any signs of debris. We can only presume he was successful in fleeing from us."

Marisha didn't seem to know how to react to that. "Oh" was all she said.

"I know that you would have liked a sense of closure on this," said Janeway, stepping to the side and turning off the forcefield. She gestured that the V'enah could now step safely through.

"And yet, perhaps it is a good thing," said Marisha, surprising Janeway with the maturity of that response. "What would we have done with him? Killed him ourselves? That goes against everything I believe in, and is not the way I wish to begin my new life. Kept him prisoner? He was a persuasive man, from what I can determine, and he might have been a powerful symbol for some who still hate my people. No, Captain. I have a great faith in destiny, even though I know I can actively shape it myself. It is best that Arkathi is just gone. If he returns, we will be stronger. We know what he is. We can deal with him then."

Janeway was beginning to see just what kind of charisma this woman possessed, and understood why Seven had been so adamant in her defense of the former slave.

"You're a very wise woman, Marisha," she said.

Marisha didn't seem to know how to respond. Finally, she smiled hesitantly. "If I am wise, then that wisdom was bought at a cost, Captain."

"Indeed it was. But it would seem that the Todanian who has filled Arkathi's footsteps is also wise. Sook has had no part in Arkathi's schemes, and is anxious to welcome you back to the ship. He wants to explore working with the V'enah on an equal basis."

"Sook," repeated Marisha, smiling fully now. "I know Sook. He is a good man, a man of his word. He has been kind to us in the past. This is a good thing, Captain. A very good thing. Will we be returned to our ship, then?"

"Not just yet. We'll rendezvous with the entire caravan at the designated planet shortly, and then you'll be free to transport over. In the meantime," Janeway continued, "we'd be honored to treat you as our guests. With the strange goings-on with the gateways, I'm afraid I have Seven of Nine busy in astrometrics, but Lieutenant Andropov will be happy to escort you to your quarters until your ship arrives. I'd appreciate it if you would remain there and not move about the ship, considering the circumstances, but please note that's a request, not an order." She didn't want Marisha to feel as though she was simply trading one sort of prison for another, more comfortable one.

Marisha understood and nodded. "Things are still quite chaotic. Certainly we have no wish to further complicate the situation. We will be happy indeed to stay in the assigned quarters and wait for your orders. Captain, I . . . there are no words to express my gratitude. Thank you for believing in us enough to challenge Arkathi."

"You're very welcome. And it's Seven who should get the credit. You'll get a chance to thank her when this is all finally straightened out."

As Janeway watched the eleven V'enah move slowly into true freedom for the first time in their lives, she wondered when things really would be finally straightened out. She took a breath, then went to her other batch of, if not quite prisoners, people who were certainly not yet free.

"I don't appreciate your attacking my crewman when you know you were being held for your own safety," she told the Hirogen Alpha a few moments later.

He regarded her coolly. "I would have felt safer aboard my own ship. Your crewman was not permanently damaged."

"Fortunately, no." She sighed. "You've been completely cleared. It turns out that Sinimar Arkathi was behind everything. He killed the Kuluuk for their supplies, then tried to make it seem as though the Hirogen had done it. When the V'enah, the slave race aboard his ship, had an uprising, Arkathi turned that to his advantage too. It was very convenient for him to eliminate any who knew about the Kuluuk murders and who might be tempted to talk, and put the blame on Marisha and her fellow slaves."

"A coward of the lowest sort," growled the Alpha,

his voice quavering with disgust. "I assume you blasted him out of the sky."

"Actually, we don't know what happened to him. We were all distracted because at one point, the gateways went completely offline. That was when the power went out a while ago. We lost everything, and apparently, many other ships did as well. We're all heading for a class-M planet at top speed in case it happens again. We'd rather be stuck where we can live than float forever in a dead ship."

"Agreed," said the Alpha, "but Arkathi is gone?"

"Disappeared. He could have used the opportunity to employ some kind of device we don't know about that would permit him to escape undetected. Or his pod could have been destroyed by the power drain somehow. I'm sorry, but we just don't know."

"I see." His voice was flat.

Janeway went on to explain their present situation, mentioning the Ones Who Will Not Be Named and their timely intervention, and concluding by saying, "We'll return you to your vessel once it reaches orbit around the planet. In the meantime, please stay in your quarters if you wouldn't mind. Do I have to put a guard there?"

The Alpha cocked his head and looked at her with an expression she couldn't quite decipher. "Not at all, Captain. We have no wish to inconvenience you further. We will wait."

There was nothing ominous in the words, and yet Janeway felt a chill chase up and down her spine. "Thank you. We'll notify you immediately when you may transport back to your vessel."

* * *

225

They were the first to reach orbit around the planet, and when Janeway returned to the bridge, she found everyone looking grim.

"Status," she snapped, bracing herself.

"The gateways are going offline again," said Chakotay. "One by one, this time. The power drain is subtle, but it's there. Not even our telepathic friends in engineering are being of much help."

Forcing herself to sound calm, Janeway said, "It would seem we got here just in time."

"And there's another thing," said Chakotay, exchanging glances with Tuvok. "There's a gateway on the planet. It just opened about a minute ago."

"Is it going offline too?"

"No, it's stable, for the moment. But Captain . . . the frequency resonance is identical to the one we encountered on the R-and-R planet. Where you found the dog."

Janeway's whole body quivered with shock. "You're joking," she said softly, glancing at Tuvok. He confirmed Chakotay's words with a nod. "But that can't be! Every single gateway had a different frequency resonance. The odds of them being duplicated must be staggering!"

"There is only one explanation," said Tuvok. "The gateway on the planet is the same gateway as the one we first encountered."

"But how? Why? Why is the same gateway appearing right here, right now?" She didn't want to answer her own question, but she thought she knew the answer. That gateway had been waiting for them, for this moment. When she didn't go through with Fluffy the first time—and now she recalled the almost unbearable yearning she had had to enter—it waited until *Voyager* had come here, now, its power draining steadily and there was no other option than to . . .

"Ships approaching, Captain," said Paris. Janeway realized she had been staring at her hands clenched tightly in her lap. She looked up to see several ships take up orbit around the planet. Even as she watched, one of the gateways in the distance flashed its rainbow hue, then closed.

"Our power has dropped six percent," said Tuvok.

"Captain!" yelled Paris. She saw it now, too. One of the ships had broken orbit and was now racing madly for one of the remaining gateways.

"Kim, hail them," she cried. Even as she spoke, she knew it was too late. The gateway for which the ship was making began to flash its rainbow lights and, before her horrified gaze, shut down.

The ship was caught half in, half out.

It was severed quite neatly. There was no fire, no jagged edges. "Lock on to all life signs and beam them aboard!" Janeway ordered.

"Got them," said Kim. "Only about twenty."

More ships were arriving. They were hailing *Voyager* now as they watched their only means of ever returning home closing slowly, one by one.

"Captain," said Kim. "I've got eight commanders wanting to speak with you. Who shall I put through?"

Janeway made her decision. "None of them," she stated, tilting her chin up. "Broadcast this message, Mr. Kim. Attention caravan, this is Captain Janeway. It appears as though all the gateways are closing, singly. With each one that closes, a greater power drain is put on many of our vessels. I can come to but one conclusion: that when the last gateway closes, we will effectively be drained of power. All the people on the remaining ships can live in a class-M environment. I advise all vessels to prepare to evacuate. I have one last avenue I wish to explore. I will contact you shortly and give the orders to evacuate if this last avenue bears no fruit. Janeway out."

Chakotay stared at Janeway, at the clean profile and the straight back. He knew what she was going to do. Even as he watched, mentally willing her not to say the words, she turned to him and spoke them.

"I'm going through."

Chakotay's heart sank. He had been afraid of this. He knew her too well. He opened his mouth to protest, but Janeway continued.

"If something isn't done soon, *Voyager* will be dead in the water—so to speak. But these gateways . . . Chakotay, there's something very deliberate about them. I know they've got to be artificial constructs. And if there is a door, a door created by someone for the purpose of going through it . . . well, then there might be someone on the other side of that door we can talk to. Maybe I'll be able to find some answers, come back with a solution. Maybe not. But I'll never know if I don't go through."

She was right, and he knew it. But he didn't have to like it.

"You shouldn't go through by yourself," he said, though again he knew what her answer would be.

She smiled oddly. "I'm not going through by my-self. I'm taking Fluffy with me."

"What? Why?"

"The readings are exactly the same as the door-way through which Barkley . . . whatever his name is . . . came the first time. It stands to reason that whatever is on the other side of that door is his home. And if he can exist there, so can I. It's actu-ally safer than you might think. At least we know I won't be walking into some other dimension."

"But we don't know that!" Chakotay protested. "We don't know anything for certain."

She smiled sadly, her eyes locked with his. "Which is precisely why I have to go through. And why I can't risk taking anyone with me. I will take Tuvok to the planet with me, but not through that gate. I have to go alone."

Gently, she placed her hand on his and continued. "I owe it not only to everyone on this ship, but everyone on all those ships out there. They're all just like us, Chakotay. They want a way home. And the pain is still fresh to them, still raw. They still have connections back home that are alive and thriving. They deserve to get home, just like we do. Maybe even more than we do, because they still have a chance to pick up their lives right where they left off. If there are answers on the other side, you bet I'll find them. I'll find them for all of us." The smile grew. "And at the very least, I can see to it that Fluffy gets home."

He had nothing to say to that. He didn't trust his voice enough to speak.

* * *

An hour later, Janeway entered the transporter room. The animal whose appearance had heralded the whole strange adventure was in her arms, eyes half closed and panting happily. Ensign Campbell stood at the controls, her eyes enormous in her pale, pretty face. Janeway knew what she was thinking— what they were all thinking, including the captain herself. Danger was nothing new to this crew. But seldom had they had the chance to think about things, to walk away from a decision like this. There was nothing certain about the situation save its uncertainty.

Tuvok and Chakotay were there, as she had requested, one on the platform, the other standing beside Campbell. They stood rigidly at attention, not meeting her eyes at first.

"Gentlemen," she said, feigning a confidence she did not feel. "If all goes well, I'll be back shortly. And with any luck, I'll have some information we can all put to use in our quest to return home. If not, I've left instructions in my room for each of you. Some personal comments as well." Playfully she punched Tuvok's arm. "I know you don't want to hear all that emotional stuff, Tuvok. Tough."

"The ship and I will be monitoring you at all times," said Tuvok. His reaction to her comments.

"For all the good that will do you," said Janeway. "You will recall we lost contact with the probe the minute I tossed it through this same gateway the first time."

"The outcome may be different," said Tuvok stubbornly. Janeway's vision blurred for a second. She recognized the Vulcan's attitude for what it was—as much of a gesture of caring as he would permit himself.

"Anything's possible," she told him. She looked up at Chakotay. Oddly, it was safer to show affection to the sometimes frosty Vulcan than to the warmly human Chakotay. "You're in charge, Commander Chakotay. You've got more than just *Voyager* to worry about right now. I know I leave them all in capable hands."

Now, finally, he did look down at her. He stretched out a big hand to rub Fluffy/Barkley's head. "I'll take care of them just as you would, Captain," he said, and that was all he needed to say.

Without another word, Janeway turned and stepped lightly up onto the transporter beside Tuvok. "Energize," she told Campbell.

She materialized on the planet, and was again struck by the similarity to Earth. Five meters straight ahead, the gateway yawned open. For a moment, Janeway allowed herself to absorb the scene. It was almost magical, surreal; the strange gateway, its interior utterly black and completely unknown, standing against the lush, waving grasses of this world.

Fluffy/Barkley began to squirm in her arms. Heartened, Janeway held him a little closer. "Not long now, little fellow," she murmured to him. Louder, she said, "Janeway to *Voyager.*"

"Reading you loud and clear, Captain," came Chakotay's voice. "Your signal's strong."

"That probably won't last," said Janeway. "I'm directly in front of the gateway. Fluffy seems anxious to go through. I'm going to take that as a good sign."

"I can detect nothing beyond the door, Captain,"

said Tuvok, in a warning voice. "I do not know if I will be able to assist you if you encounter problems."

"I understand. But you'll be right here in case I do need you." She paused, swallowed, then said calmly, "I'm going in."

Head held high, shoulders squared, Captain Kathryn Janeway stepped over the threshold, not knowing what lay beyond.

On the bridge of the starship *Voyager,* Ensign Harry Kim took a swift breath. At Chakotay's questioning look, he said in a low voice, "She's gone."

To be continued . . .

Look for STAR TREK fiction from Pocket Books

Star Trek®: The Original Series

Star Trek: The Next Generation®

Star Trek: Voyager®

Star Trek®: New Frontier

Star Trek®: Starfleet Corps of Engineers (eBooks)

#1 • *The Belly of the Beast* • Dean Wesley Smith
#2 • *Fatal Error* • Keith R.A. DeCandido
#3 • *Hard Crash* • Christie Golden
#4 • *Interphase, Book One* • Dayton Ward & Kevin Dilmore
#5 • *Interphase, Book Two* • Dayton Ward & Kevin Dilmore
#6 • *Cold Fusion* • Keith R.A. Decandido
#7 • *Invincible, Book One* • Keith R.A. Decandido and David Mack
#8 • *Invincible, Book Two* • Keith R.A. Decandido and David Mack

Star Trek®: Invasion!

#1 • *First Strike* • Diane Carey
#2 • *The Soldiers of Fear* • Dean Wesley Smith & Kristine Kathryn Rusch
#3 • *Time's Enemy* • L.A. Graf
#4 • *The Final Fury* • Dafydd ab Hugh
Invasion! Omnibus • various

Star Trek®: Day of Honor

#1 • *Ancient Blood* • Diane Carey
#2 • *Armageddon Sky* • L.A. Graf
#3 • *Her Klingon Soul* • Michael Jan Friedman
#4 • *Treaty's Law* • Dean Wesley Smith & Kristine Kathryn Rusch
The Television Episode • Michael Jan Friedman
Day of Honor Omnibus • various

Star Trek®: The Captain's Table

#1 • *War Dragons* • L.A. Graf
#2 • *Dujonian's Hoard* • Michael Jan Friedman
#3 • *The Mist* • Dean Wesley Smith & Kristine Kathryn Rusch
#4 • *Fire Ship* • Diane Carey
#5 • *Once Burned* • Peter David
#6 • *Where Sea Meets Sky* • Jerry Oltion
The Captain's Table Omnibus • various

Star Trek®: The Dominion War

#1 • *Behind Enemy Lines* • John Vornholt
#2 • *Call to Arms...* • Diane Carey
#3 • *Tunnel Through the Stars* • John Vornholt
#4 • *...Sacrifice of Angels* • Diane Carey

Star Trek®: Section 31

Rogue • Andy Mangels & Michael A. Martin
Shadow • Dean Wesley Smith & Kristine Kathryn Rusch
Cloak • S. D. Perry
Abyss • Dean Weddle & Jeffrey Lang

Star Trek®: Gateways

#1 • *One Small Step* • Susan Wright
#2 • *Chainmail* • Diane Carey

Star Trek®: The Badlands

#1 • Susan Wright
#2 • Susan Wright

Star Trek®: Dark Passions

#1 • Susan Wright
#2 • Susan Wright

Star Trek® Omnibus Editions

Invasion! Omnibus • various
Day of Honor Omnibus • various
The Captain's Table Omnibus • various
Star Trek: Odyssey • William Shatner with Judith and Garfield Reeves-
 Stevens

Other Star Trek® Fiction

Legends of the Ferengi • Ira Steven Behr & Robert Hewitt Wolfe
Strange New Worlds, vols. I, II, III, and IV • Dean Wesley Smith, ed.
Adventures in Time and Space • Mary P. Taylor
Captain Proton: Defender of the Earth • D.W. "Prof" Smith
New Worlds, New Civilizations • Michael Jan Friedman
The Lives of Dax • Marco Palmieri, ed.
The Klingon Hamlet • Wil'yam Shex'pir
Enterprise Logs • Carol Greenburg, ed.

HAPPY HOLIDAYS
FROM NEELIX AND

KOMAR COOKIES from the STAR TREK COOKBOOK

When I was courting Kes, I was a lot leaner—in fact I spent a few years as a swimsuit model on Talax—but now I've filled out, and why not? I always say, "Beware the skinny cook." One of the reasons I've gained a little weight is this dish created by the Komar. They live in a nebula and feed off the neural energy of other species. They're not real nice, but they make a great cookie. They don't bake theirs—they zap the dough with a magnetodynamic TL 5 solar-photox blast, but you don't have to do that, unless you know how. The dough is made from rattle fern caviar, Turian stardust, and Betelgeuse butter. The Komar also add wineworm blood, but I think this detracts from the already intense taste. ADAPTED FOR 20th CENTURY KITCHENS

1 cup all purpose flour
1/2 cup (1 stick) of butter
1/2 cup light brown sugar
1 egg
1 egg white
1 tsp. cinnamon
1/2 tsp. vanilla extract
1/4 tsp. salt
granulated sugar, as needed for coating
raspberry or straw-berry jelly or preserves

NLXI

HAPPY HOLIDAYS
FROM NEELIX AND

Cream the butter and brown sugar and beat in the whole egg, flour, vanilla, cinnamon, and salt. Roll the dough and chill in your refrigerator for about 15 minutes while you preheat your oven to 375 degrees. When the dough has been chilled, break off individual 1-inch pieces and roll into small balls. Lightly beat egg white in a small bowl until it's slightly frothy, not membranous. Next, fill a small bowl with granulated sugar. Coat the balls in the egg white and then roll them in sugar to coat them. Now arrange them on a flat greased baking sheet and make a slight impression in each with your finger—or you can use the broad end of a chopstick or even a thimble. Drop a small amount of raspberry or strawberry jelly or preserves into each depression and close over the depression with the cookie dough. Bake at 375 degrees for about 10 minutes. Allow to cool before serving.

These make incredible Christmas and holiday gifts and can become a holiday tradition. Wrap them in fancy paper and bows for friends and neighbors. Yields two dozen cookies.

THE STAR TREK®COOKBOOK
Star Trek cuisine for the earthbound chef!

STAR TREK VOYAGER®

CHRISTIE GOLDEN

#6: The Murdered Sun

When sensors indicate a possible wormhole nearby, Captain Janeway is eager to investigate, hoping to find a shortcut home. Instead, she discovers a star system being systematically pillaged by the warlike Akerians. *Voyager* may have no choice but to challenge the agressors—but who knows what unexpected dangers lurk beneath the murdered sun?

#14: Marooned

When an alien pirate abducts Kes, *Voyager* takes off in hot pursuit, but an ion storm forces Captain Janeway and the rescue team to crash on an unknown world. Now they must embark on a hazardous trek in search of a way off the planet, while Chakotay confronts an enemy fleet in the depths of space.

#16: Seven of Nine

Once she was Annika Hansen, a human child. Now she is Seven of Nine, a unique mixture of human biology and Borg technology. Cut off from the collective and forced to join *Voyager*'s crew, Seven must come to grips with her new environment —and her own lost individuality.

CGBL